James Frederick

James Frederick Ferrier

by Elizabeth Sanderson Haldane

INTRODUCTION

Mr. Oliphant Smeaton has asked me to write a few words of preface to this little book. If I try, it is only because I am old enough to have had the privilege of knowing some of those who were most closely associated with Ferrier.

When I sat at the feet of Professor Campbell Fraser in the Metaphysics classroom at Edinburgh in 1875, Ferrier's writings were being much read by us students. The influence of Sir William Hamilton was fast crumbling in the minds of young men who felt rather than saw that much lay beyond it. We were still engrossed with the controversy, waged in books which now, alas! sell for a tenth of their former price, about the Conditioned and the Unconditioned. We still worked at Reid, Hamilton, and Mansel. But the attacks of Mill on the one side, and of Ferrier and Dr. Stirling on the other, were slowly but surely withdrawing our interest. Ferrier had pointed out a path which seemed to lead us in the direction of Germany if we would escape from Mill, and Stirling was urging us in the same sense. It was not merely that Ferrier had written books. He had died more than ten years earlier, but his personality was still a living influence. Echoes of his words came to us through Grant and Sellar. Outside the University, men like Blackwood and Makgill made us feel what a power he had been. But that was not all for at least some of us. Mrs. Ferrier had removed to Edinburgh—and I endorse all that my sister says of her rare quality. She lived in a house in Torphichen Street, which was the resort of those attracted, not only by the memory of her husband, but by her own great gifts. She was an old lady and an invalid. But though she could not move from her chair, paralysis had not dimmed her mental powers. She was a true daughter of 'Christopher North.' I doubt whether I have seen her rival in quickness, her superior I never saw. She could talk admirably to those sitting near her, and yet follow and join in the conversation of another group at the end of the room. She could adapt herself to everyone—to the shy and awkward student of eighteen, who like myself was too much in awe of her to do more unhelped than answer, and to the distinguished men of letters who came from every quarter attracted by her reputation for brilliance. The words of no one could be more incisive, the words of no one were habitually more kind than hers. She had known everybody. She forgot nobody. In those days the relation between Literature and the Parliament House, if less close than it had been, was more apparent than it is to-day, and distinguished Scottish judges and advocates mingled in the afternoon in the drawing-room, where she sat in a great arm-chair, with such men as Sellar and Stevenson and Grant and Shairp and Tulloch. But her personality was the supreme bond.

Those days are over, and with them has passed away much of what stimulated one to read in the *Institutes* or the *Philosophical Remains*. But for the historian of British philosophy Ferrier continues as a prominent figure. He it was who first did, what Stirling and Green did again at a stage later on—make a serious appeal to thoughtful people to follow no longer the shallow rivulets down which the teaching of the great German thinkers had trickled to them, but to seek the sources. If as a guide to those sources we do not look on him to-day as adequate, we are not the less under a deep obligation to him for having been the pioneer of later guides. What Ferrier wrote about forty years ago has now become readily accessible, and what has been got by going there is in process of rapid and complete assimilation. The opinions which were in 1856 regarded by the authorities of the Free and United Presbyterian Churches as disqualifying Ferrier for the opportunity of influencing the mind of the youth of Edinburgh, from the Chair of Logic and Metaphysics in succession to Sir William Hamilton, are regarded by the present generation of Presbyterians as the main reliable bulwark against the attacks of unbelievers. If one may judge by the essays in the recent volume called *Lux Mundi*, the same phenomenon displays itself among the young High Church party in England. The Time-Spirit is fond of revenges.

But even for others than the historians of the movement of Thought the books of Ferrier remain attractive. There is about them a certain atmosphere in which everything seems alive and fresh. Their author was no Dryasdust. He was a living human being, troubled as we are troubled, and interested in the things which interest us. He spoke to us, not from the skies, but from among a crowd of his fellow human beings, and we feel that he was one of ourselves. As such it is good that a memorial of him should be placed where it may easily be seen.

R. B. Haldane.

CHAPTER I

EARLY LIFE

It may be a truism, but it is none the less a fact, that it is not always he of whom the world hears most who influences most deeply the thought of the age in which he lives. The name of James Frederick Ferrier is little heard of beyond the comparatively small circle of philosophic thinkers who reverence his memory and do their best to keep it green: to others it is a name of little import—one among a multitude at a time when Scotland had many sons rising up to call her blessed, and not perhaps one of the most notable of these. And yet, could we but estimate the value of work accomplished in the higher sphere of thought as we estimate it in the other regions of practical work—an impossibility, of course—we might be disposed to modify our views, and accord our praises in very different quarters from those in which they are usually bestowed.

James Ferrier wrote no popular books; he came before the public comparatively little; he made no effort to reconcile religion with philosophy on the one hand, or to propound theories startling in their unorthodoxy on the other. And still we may claim for him a place—and an honourable place—amongst the other Famous Scots, for the simple reason that after a long century of wearisome reiteration of tiresome platitudes—platitudes which had lost their original meaning even to the utterers of them, and which had become misleading to those who heard and thought they understood—Ferrier had the courage to strike out new lines for himself, to look abroad for new inspiration, and to hand on these inspirations to those who could work them into a truly national philosophy.

In Scotland, where, in spite of politics, traditions are honoured to a degree unknown to most other countries, family and family associations count for much; and in these James Ferrier was rich. His father was a Writer to the Signet, John Ferrier by name, whose sister was the famous Scottish novelist, Susan Ferrier, authoress of *The Inheritance*, *Destiny*, and *Marriage*. Susan Ferrier did for high life in Scotland what Gait achieved for the humbler ranks of society, and attained to considerable eminence in the line of fiction which she adopted. Her works are still largely read, have recently been republished, and in their day were greatly admired by no less an authority than Sir Walter Scott, himself a personal friend of the authoress.[1] Ferrier's grandfather, James Ferrier, also a Writer to the Signet, was a man of great energy of character. He acted in a business capacity for many years both to the Duke of Argyle of the time and to various branches of the Clan Campbell: it was, indeed, through the influence of the Duke that he obtained the appointment which he held of Principal Clerk of Session. James Ferrier, like his daughter, was on terms of intimate friendship with Sir Walter Scott, with whom he likewise was a colleague in office. Scott alludes to him in his Journal as 'Uncle Adam,' the name of a character in Miss Ferrier's *Inheritance*, drawn, as she herself acknowledges, from her father. He died in 1829, at which time Scott writes of him: 'Honest old Mr. Ferrier is dead, at extreme old age. I confess I should not like to live so long. He was a man with strong passions and strong prejudices, but with generous and manly sentiments at the same time.' James Ferrier's wife, Miss Coutts, was remarkable for her beauty: a large family was born to her, the eldest son of whom was James Frederick Ferrier's father. Young Ferrier, the subject of this sketch, used frequently to dine with his grandfather at his house in Morningside, where Susan Ferrier acted in the capacity of hostess; and it is easy to imagine the bright talk which would take place on these occasions, and the impression which must have been made upon the lad, both then and after he attained to manhood; for Miss Ferrier survived until 1854. In later life, indeed, her wit was said to be somewhat caustic, and she was possibly dreaded by her younger friends and relatives as much as she was respected; but this, to do her justice, was partly owing to infirmities. She was at anyrate keenly interested in the fortunes of her nephew, to whom she was in the habit of alluding as 'the last of the metaphysicians'— scarcely, perhaps, a very happy title for one who was somewhat of an iconoclast, and began a new era rather than concluded an old.

James Frederick Ferrier's mother, Margaret Wilson, was a sister of Professor John Wilson—the 'Christopher North' of immortal memory, whose daughter he was afterwards to marry. Margaret Ferrier was a woman of striking personal beauty. Her features were perfect in their symmetry, as is shown in a lovely miniature, painted by Saunders, a well-known miniature painter of the day, now in the possession of Professor Ferrier's son, her grandson. Many of these personal charms descended to James Ferrier, whose well-cut features bore considerable resemblance to his mother's. And his close connection with the

Wilson family had the result of bringing the young man into association with whatever was best in literature and art. While yet a boy, we are told, he sat upon Sir Walter's knee; the Ettrick Shepherd had told him tales and recited Border ballads; while Lockhart took the trouble to draw pictures, as he only could, to amuse the child.

In surroundings such as these James Frederick Ferrier was born on the 16th day of June 1808, his birthplace being Heriot Row, in the new town of Edinburgh—a street which has been made historic to us by the recollections of another child who lived there long years afterwards, and who left the grey city of his birth to die far off in an island in the Pacific. But of Ferrier's child-life we know nothing: whether he played at 'tig' or 'shinty' with the children in the adjoining gardens, or climbed Arthur's Seat, or tried to scale the 'Cats' Nick' in the Salisbury Crags close by; or whether he was a grave boy, 'holding at' his lessons, or reading other books that interested him, in preference to his play. Ferrier did not dwell on these things or talk much of his youth; or if he did so, his words have been forgotten. What we do know are the barest facts: that his second name was given him in consideration of his father's friendship with Lord Frederick Campbell, Lord Clerk Register of Scotland; that his first name, as is usual in Scotland for an elder son, was his paternal grandfather's; and that he was sent to live with the Rev. Dr. Duncan, the parish minister of Ruthwell, in Dumfriesshire, to receive his early education. Dr. Duncan of Ruthwell was a man of considerable ability and energy of character, though not famous in any special sphere of learning. He is well known, however, in the south of Scotland as the originator of Savings Banks there, and his works on the Seasons bear evidence of an interest in the natural world. At anyrate the time passed in Dumfriesshire would appear to have left pleasant recollections; for when Ferrier in later life alluded to it, it was with every indication of gratitude for the instruction which he received. He kept up his friendship with the sons of his instructor as years went on, and always expressed himself as deeply attached to the place where a happy childhood had been passed. Nor was learning apparently neglected, for Ferrier began his Latin studies at Ruthwell, and there first learned—an unusual lesson for so young a boy—to delight in the reading of the Latin poets, and of Virgil and Ovid in particular. After leaving Ruthwell, he attended the High School of Edinburgh, the great Grammar School of the metropolis, which was, however, soon to have a rival in another day school set up in the western part of the rapidly growing town; and then he was sent to school at Greenwich, where he was placed under the care of Dr. Burney, a nephew of the famous Fanny Burney, afterwards Madame d'Arblay. From school, as the manner of the time was, the boy passed to the University of Edinburgh at the age of seventeen,—older really than was customary in his day,—and here he remained for the two sessions 1825-26 and 1826-27, or until he was old enough to matriculate at Oxford. At Edinburgh, Ferrier distinguished himself in the class of Moral Philosophy, and carried off the prize of the year for a poem which was looked upon as giving promise of literary power afterwards fulfilled. His knowledge of Latin and Greek were considered good (the standard might not have been very high), but in mathematics he was nowhere. At Oxford he was entered in 1828 as a 'gentleman-commoner' at Magdalen College, the College of his future father-in-law, John Wilson. A gentleman-commoner of Magdalen in the earlier half of the century is not suggestive of severe mental exercise,[2] and from the very little one can gather from tradition—for contemporaries and friends have naturally passed away—James Ferrier was no exception to the common rule. That he rode is very clear; the College was an expensive one, and he was probably inclined to be extravagant. Tradition speaks of his pelting the deer in Magdalen Park with eggs; but as to further distinction in more intellectual lines, record does not tell. In this respect he presents a contrast to his predecessor at Oxford, and friend of later days, Sir William Hamilton, whose monumental learning created him a reputation while still an undergraduate. Sir Roundell Palmer, afterwards Lord Selborne, was a contemporary of Ferrier's at Oxford; Sheriff Campbell Smith was at the bar of the House of Lords acting as Palmer's junior the day after Ferrier's death, and Sir Roundell told him that he remembered Ferrier well at College; he described him as 'careless about University work,' but as writing clever verses, several of which he repeated with considerable gusto. Of other friends the names alone are preserved, William Edward Collins, afterwards Collins-Wood of Keithick, Perthshire, who died in 1877, and J. P. Shirley of Ettington Park, in Warwickshire;[3] but what influences were brought to bear upon him by his University life, or whether his interest in philosophical pursuits were in any way aroused during his time at College, we have no means of telling. A later friend, Henry Inglis, wrote of these early days: 'My friendship with Ferrier began about the time he was leaving Oxford, or immediately after he had left it—I should say about 1830 or thereabout. At that University I don't think he did anything more remarkable than contracting a large tailor's bill; which annoyed him for many years afterwards. At that time he was a wonderfully handsome, intellectual-looking young man,—a tremendous "swell" from top to toe, and with his hair hanging down over his shoulders.' Though later on in life this last characteristic was not so marked, Ferrier's photographs show his hair still fairly long and brushed off a finely-modelled square forehead, such as is usually associated with strongly developed intellectual faculties.

It is known that Ferrier took his Bachelor's degree in 1832, and that he had by that time managed to acquire a very tolerable knowledge of the classics and begun to study philosophy, so that his time could not have been entirely idle. For the rest, he probably passed happily through his years at College, as many others have done before and after him, without allowing more weighty cares to dwell upon his mind. Another friend of after days, the late Principal Tulloch, after noting the fact that Oxford had not then developed the philosophic spirit which in recent years has marked her schools, and which had not then taken root any more than the High Church movement which preceded it, goes on: 'It may be doubted, indeed, whether Oxford exercised any definite intellectual influence on Professor Ferrier. He had imbibed his love for the Latin poets before he went there, and his devotion to Greek philosophy was an after-growth with which he never associated his Magdalen studies. To one who visited the College with him many years afterwards, and to whom he pointed out with admiration its noble walks and trees, his associations with the place seemed to be mainly those of amusement. There is reason to think that few of those who knew him at Magdalen would have afterwards recognised him in the laborious student at St. Andrews, who for weeks together would scarcely cross the threshold of his study; and yet to all who knew him well, there was nevertheless a clear connection between the gay gownsman and the hard-working Professor.'

In 1832, Ferrier became an advocate at Edinburgh, but it does not appear that he had any serious idea of practising at the Bar. This is the period at which we know that the passion for metaphysical speculation laid hold of him,—a passion which is unintelligible and inexplicable to those who do not share in it,—and as Ferrier could not clearly say in what direction this was leading him, as far as practical life was concerned, he probably deemed it best to attach himself to a profession which left much scope to the adopter of it, to strike out lines of his own. What led Ferrier to determine to spend some months of the year 1834 at Heidelberg it would be extremely interesting to know. The friend first quoted writes: 'I cannot tell of the influences under which he devoted himself to metaphysics. My opinion is that there were none, but that he was a philosopher born. He attached himself at once to the fellowship of Sir William Hamilton, to whom he was introduced by a common friend—I think the late Mr. Ludovic Colquhoun. I know that he looked on Sir William at that time as his master.'

Probably the friendship with Hamilton simply arose from the natural attraction which two sympathetic spirits feel to one another. It is clear that at this time Ferrier's bent was towards metaphysics, and that, as Mr. Inglis says, this bent was born with him and was only beginning to find its natural outlet; therefore it would be very natural to suppose that acquaintance would be sought with one who was at this time in the zenith of his powers, and whose writings in the *Edinburgh Review* were exciting liveliest interest. A casual acquaintanceship between the young man of three-and-twenty and the matured philosopher twenty years his senior soon ripened into a friendship, not perhaps common between two men so different in age. It is perhaps more remarkable considering the differences in opinion on philosophical questions which soon arose between the two; for it is just as difficult for those whose point of view is fundamentally opposed on speculative questions to carry on an intercourse concerning their pursuits which shall be both friendly and unconstrained, as for two political opponents to discuss vital questions of policy without any undercurrent of self-restraint, when they start from entirely opposite principles. Most likely had the two been actually contemporaries it might not have been so easy, but as it was, the younger man started with, and preserved, the warmest feelings to his senior; and even in his criticisms he expresses himself in the strongest terms of gratitude: 'He (Hamilton) has taught those who study him to *think*, and he must take the consequences, whether they think in unison with himself or not. We conceive, however, that even those who differ from him most, would readily own that to his instructive disquisitions they were indebted for at least half of all they know of philosophy.' And in the appendix to the *Institutes*, written soon after Sir William's death, Ferrier says: 'Morally and intellectually, Sir William Hamilton was among the greatest of the great. A simpler and a grander nature never arose out of darkness into human life; a truer and a manlier character God never made. For years together scarcely a day passed in which I was not in his company for hours, and never on this earth may I expect to live such happy hours again. I have learned more from him than from all other philosophers put together; more, both as regards what I assented to and what I dissented from.' It was this open and free discussion of all questions that came before them— discussion in which there must have been much difference of opinion freely expressed on both sides, that made these evenings spent in Manor Place, where the Hamiltons, then a recently married couple, had lately settled, so delightful to young Ferrier. He had individuality and originality enough not to be carried away by the arguments used by so great an authority and so learned a man as his friend was reckoned, and then as later he constantly expressed his regret that powers so great had been devoted to the service of a philosophic system—that of Reid—of which Ferrier so thoroughly disapproved. But at the same time he hardly dared to expect that the labours of a lifetime could be set aside at the bidding of a man so much his junior, and to say the truth it is doubtful whether Hamilton ever fully grasped his opponent's point of view. Still, Ferrier tells us that from first to last his whole intercourse with Sir William Hamilton was marked with more pleasure and less pain than ever attended his intercourse with any human being, and after Hamilton was gone he cherished that memory with affectionate esteem. A touching account is given in Sir William's life of how during that terrible illness which so sadly impaired his powers and nearly took his life, Ferrier might be seen pacing to and fro on the street opposite his bedroom window during the whole anxious night, watching for indications of his condition, yet unwilling to intrude on the attendants, and unable to tear himself from the spot where his friend was possibly passing through the last agony. Such friendship is honourable to both men concerned.

Perhaps, then, it was this intercourse with kindred spirits (for many such were in the habit of gathering at the Professor's house) that caused Ferrier finally to determine to make philosophy the pursuit of his life—this combined, it may be, with the interest in letters which he could not fail to derive from his own immediate circle. He was in constant communication with Susan Ferrier, his aunt, who encouraged his literary bent to the utmost of her power. Then Professor Wilson, his uncle, though of a very different character from his own, attracted him by his brightness and wit—a brightness which he says he can hardly bring before himself, far less communicate to others who had not known him. Perhaps, as the same friend quoted before suggests, the attraction was partly due to another source. He says: 'How Ferrier got on with Wilson I never could divine; unless it were through the bright eyes of his daughter. Wilson and Ferrier seemed to me as opposite as the poles; the one all poetry, the other all prose. But the youth probably yielded to the mature majesty and genius of the man. Had they met on equal terms I don't think they could have agreed for ten minutes. As it was, they had serious differences at times, which, however, I believe were all ultimately and happily adjusted.'

The visits to his uncle's home, and the attractive young lady whom he there met, must have largely contributed to Ferrier's happiness in these years of mental fermentation. Such times come in many men's lives when youth is turning into manhood, and powers are wakening up within that seem as though they would lead us we know not whither. And so it may have been with Ferrier. But he was endowed with considerable calmness and self-command, combined with a confidence in his powers sufficient to carry him through many difficulties that might otherwise have got the better of him. Wilson's home, Elleray, near the Lake of Windermere, was the centre of a circle of brilliant stars. Ferrier recollected, while still a lad of seventeen years of age, meeting there at one time, in the summer of 1825, Scott, Wordsworth, Lockhart, and Canning, a conjunction difficult to beat.[4] Once more, we are told, and on a sadder occasion, he came into association with the greatest Scottish novelist. 'It was on that gloomy voyage when the suffering man was conveyed to Leith from London, on his return from his ill-fated foreign journey. Mr. Ferrier was also a passenger, and scarcely dared to look on the almost unconscious form of one whose genius he so warmly admired.' The end was then very near.

Professor Ferrier's daughter tells us that long after, in the summer of 1856, the family went to visit the English Lakes, the centre of attraction being Elleray, Mr. Ferrier's old home and birthplace. 'The very name of Elleray breathes of poetry and romance. Our father and mother had, of course, known it in its glorious prime, when our grandfather, "Christopher North," wrestled with dalesmen, strolled in his slippers with Wordsworth to Keswick (a distance of seventeen miles), and kept his ten-oared barge in the long drawing-room of Elleray. In these days they had "rich company," and the names of Southey, Wordsworth, De Quincey, and Coleridge were to them familiar household words. The cottage my mother was born in still stands, overshadowed by a giant sycamore.'

We can easily imagine the effect which society such as this would have on a young man's mind. But more than that, the friendship with the attractive cousin, Margaret Wilson, developed into something warmer, and an engagement was finally formed, which culminated in his marriage in 1837. Not many of James Ferrier's letters to his cousin during the long engagement have been preserved; the few that are were written from Germany in 1834, the year in which he went to Heidelberg; they were addressed to Thirlstane House, near Selkirk, where Miss Wilson was residing, and they give a lively account of his adventures.

The voyage from Leith to Rotterdam, judging from the first letter written from Heidelberg, and dated August 1834, would appear to have begun in inauspicious fashion. Ferrier writes: 'I have just been here a week, and would have answered your letter sooner, had it not been that I wished to make myself tolerably well acquainted with the surrounding scenery before writing to you, and really the heat has been so overwhelming that I have been impelled to take matters leisurely, and have not even yet been able to get through so much *view-hunting* as I should have wished. What I have seen I will endeavour to describe to you. This place itself is most delightful, and the country about it is magnificent. But this, as a reviewer would say, *by way of anticipation*. Have patience, and in the meantime let me take events in their natural order, and begin by telling you I sailed from Leith on the morning of the second of this month, with no wind at all. We drifted on, I know not how, and toward evening were within gunshot of

Inchkeith; on the following morning we were in sight of the Bass, and in sight of the same we continued during the whole day. For the next two or three days we went beating up against a head-wind, which forced us to tack so much that whenever we made one mile we travelled ten, a pleasant mode of progressing, is it not? However, I had the whole ship to myself, and plenty of female society in the person of the captain's lady, who, being fond of pleasure, had chosen to diversify her monotonous existence at Leith by taking a delightful summer trip to Rotterdam, which confined her to her crib during almost the whole of our passage under the pressure of racking headaches and roaring sickness. She had a weary time of it, poor woman, and nothing could do her any good—neither spelding, cheese, nor finnan haddies, nor bacon, nor broth, nor salt beef, nor ale, nor gin, nor brandy and water, nor Epsom salts, though of one or other of these she was *aye takin'* a wee bit, or a little drop. We were nearly a week in clearing our own Firth, and did no good till we got as far as Scarborough. At this place I had serious intentions of getting ashore if possible, and making out the rest of my journey by means that were more to be depended on. Just in the nick of time, however, a fair wind sprang up, and from Scarborough we had a capital run, with little or no interruption, to the end of our voyage.' An account of a ten days' voyage which makes us thankful to be in great measure independent of the winds at sea! Holland, our traveller thinks an intolerable country to live in, and the first impressions of the Rhine are distinctly unfavourable. 'The river himself is a fine fellow, certainly, but the country through which he flows is stale, flat, though I believe, not unprofitable. The banks on either side are covered either with reeds or with a matting of rank shrubbery formed apparently out of dirty green worsted, and the continuance of it so palls upon the senses that the mind at last becomes unconscious of everything except the constant flap-flapping of the weary paddles as they go beating on, awakening the dull echoes of the sedgy shores. The eye is occasionally relieved by patches of naked sand, and now and then a stone about the size of your fist, diversifies the monotony of the scene. Occasionally, in the distance, are to be seen funny, forlorn-looking objects, trying evidently to look like trees, but whether they would really turn out to be trees on a nearer inspection is what I very much doubt.' At Cologne he had an amusing meeting with an Englishman, 'whom I at once twigged to be an Oxford man, and more, even, an Oxford tutor. There is a stiff twitch in the right shoulder of the tribe, answering to a similar one in the hip-bone on the same side, which there is no mistaking.' The tutor appears to have done valiant service in making known the traveller's wants in French to waiters, etc., though 'he spent rather too much of his time in scheming how to abridge the sixpence which, "time out of mind," has been the perquisite of Boots, doorkeepers, etc.' 'But,' he adds in excuse, 'his name was Bull, and therefore, as the authentic epitome of his countrymen, he would not fail to possess this along with the other peculiarities of Englishmen.' From Cologne, Ferrier went to Bonn, where he had an introduction to Dr. Welsh, and then proceeded up the Rhine to Mayence. He does not form a very high estimate of the beauty of the scenery. He feels 'a want of something; in fact, to my mind, there is a want of everything which makes earth, wood, and water something more than mere water, wood, and earth. We have here a constant and endless variety of imposing objects (imposing is just the word for them), but there is no variety in them, nothing but one round-backed hill after another, generally carrying their woods, when they have any, very stiffly, and when they have none presenting to the eye a surface of tawdry and squalid patchwork,' thus suggesting, in his view, a series of children's gardens—an impression often left on travellers when visiting this same country. His next letters find him settled in the University town of Heidelberg.

CHAPTER II

WANDERJAHRE—SOCIAL LIFE IN SCOTLAND—BEGINNING OF HIS LITERARY LIFE

In the present century in Germany we have seen a period of almost unparalleled literary glory succeeded by a time of great commercial prosperity and national enthusiasm. But when Ferrier visited that country in 1834 the era of its intellectual greatness had hardly passed away; some, at least, of its stars remained, and others had very recently ceased to be. Goethe had died just two years before, but Heine lived till many years afterwards; amongst the philosophers, though Kant and Fichte, of course, were long since gone, Schelling was still at work at Munich, and Hegel lived at Berlin till November of 1831, when he was cut off during an epidemic of cholera. Most of the great men had disappeared, and yet the memory of their achievements still survived, and the impetus they gave to thought could not have been lost. The traditional lines of speculation consistently carried out since Reformation days had survived war and national calamity, and it remained to be seen whether the greater tests of prosperity and success would be as triumphantly undergone.

We can imagine Ferrier's feelings when this new world opened up before him, a Scottish youth, to whom it was a new, untrodden country. It may be true that it was his literary rather than his speculative affinities that first attracted him to Germany. To form in literature he always attached the greatest value, and to the end his interest in letters was only second to his attachment to philosophy. German poetry was to him what it was to so many of the youth of the country from which it came—the expression of their deepest, and likewise of their freshest aspiration. The poetry of other countries and other tongues—English and Latin, for example—meant much to him, but that of Germany was nearest to his heart. French learning did not attract him; neither its literature nor its metaphysics and psychological method appealed to his thoughtful, analytic mind; but in Germany he found a nation which had not as yet resigned its interest in things of transcendental import in favour of what pertained to mere material welfare.

Such was the Germany into which Ferrier came in 1834. He did not, so far as we can hear, enter deeply into its social life; he visited it as a traveller, rather than as a student, and his stay in it was brief. Considering the shortness of his time there, and the circumstances of his visit, the impression that it made upon him is all the more remarkable, for it was an impression that lasted and was evident throughout all his after life. Since his day, indeed, it would be difficult to say how many young Scotsmen have been impressed in a similar way by a few months' residence at a University town in Germany. For partly owing to Ferrier's own efforts, and perhaps even more owing to the 'boom'—to use a vulgarism—brought about by Carlyle's writings, and by his first making known the marvels of German literature to the ordinary English-speaking public, who had never learned the language or tried to understand its recent history, the old traditional literary alliance between Scotland and France appeared for the time being to have broken down in favour of a similar association with its rival country, Germany. The work of Goethe was at last appreciated, nothing was now too favourable to say about its merits; philosophy was suddenly discovered to have its home in Germany, and there alone; our insularity in keeping to our antiquated methods—dryasdust, we were told, as the old ones of the schools, and perhaps as edifying—was vigorously denounced. Theology, which had hitherto found complete support from the philosophic system which acted as her handmaid, and was only tolerated as such, was naturally affected in like manner by the change; and to her credit be it said, that instead of with averted eyes looking elsewhere, as might easily have been done, she determined to face the worst, and wisely asked the question whether in her department too she had not something she could learn from a sister country across the sea. Hence a great change was brought about in the mental attitude of Scotland; but we anticipate.

Ferrier, after leaving Heidelberg, paid a short visit to Leipzig, and then for a few weeks took up his abode at Berlin. From Leipzig he writes to Miss Wilson again: 'How do you like an *epistola* dated from this great emporium of taste and letters, this culminating point of Germanism, where waggons jostle philosophy, and tobacco-impregnated air is articulated into divinest music? It is fair-time, and I did not arrive, as one usually does, a day *behind* it, but on the very day it commenced. It will last, I believe, some weeks, and during that time all business is done on the open streets, which are lined on each side with large wooden booths, and are swarming with men and merchandise of every description and from every quarter of the world. It very much resembles a *Ladies' Sale* in the Assembly Rooms (what I never saw), only the ladies here are frequently Jews with fierce beards, and have always a pipe in their mouths when not eating or drinking. As you walk along you will find the order of the day to be somewhat as follows. You first come to pipes, then shawls, then nails, then pipes, pipes again, pipes, gingerbread, dolls, then pipes, bridles, spurs, pipes, books, warming-pans, pipes, china, writing-desks, pipes again, pipes, pipes, pipes, nothing but pipes—the very pen will write nothing but pipes. Pipes, you see, decidedly carry it. I wonder they don't erect public tobacco-smoke works, lay *pipes* for it along the streets, and smoke away—a city at a time. Private families might take it in as we do gas!'

Ferrier appears to have spent a week at Frankfort before reaching his destination at Leipzig. He describes his journey there: 'At Frankfort I saw nothing worthy of note except a divine statue of Ariadne riding on a leopard. After lumbering along for two nights and two days in a clumsy diligence, I reached Leipzig two days ago. I thought that by the way I might perhaps see something worthy of mention, and accordingly sometimes put my head out of the window to look. But no—the trees, for instance, had all to a man planted their heads in the earth, and were growing with their legs upwards, just as they do with us; and as for the natives, they, on the contrary, had each of them filled a flower-pot, called a skull, full of earth, put their heads in it, and were growing *downwards*, just as the same animal does in our country; and on coming to one's recollection in the morning in a German diligence you find yourself surrounded by the same drowsy, idiotical, glazed, stained, and gummy complement of faces which might have accompanied you into Carlisle on an autumn morning after a night of travel in His Majesty's mail coach.'

Berlin impressed Ferrier by its imposing public buildings and general aspect of prosperity. It had, of course, long before reached a position of importance under the great Frederick's government, though not the importance or the size that it afterwards attained. Still, it was the centre of attraction for all classes throughout Prussia, and possessed a cultivated society in which the middle-class element was to all appearances predominant. Ferrier writes of the town: 'Of the inside of the buildings and what is to be seen there I have nothing yet to say, but their external aspect is most magnificent. Palaces, churches, mosque-like structures, spires and domes and towers all standing together, but with large spaces and fine open drives between, so that all are seen to the greatest possible advantage, conspire to form a most glorious city. At this moment a fountain which I can see from my window is playing in the middle of the square. A *jet d'eau* indeed!! It may do very well for a Frenchman to call it that, but we must call it a perfect volcano of water. A huge column goes hissing up as high as a steeple, with the speed and force of a rocket, and comes down in thunder, and little rainbows are flitting about in the showery spray. It being Sunday, every thing and person is gayer than usual. Bands are playing and soldiers are parading all through the town; everything, indeed, is military, and yet little is foppish—a statement which to English ears will sound like a direct contradiction.'

Our traveller had been given letters to certain Berlin Professors from young Blackie, afterwards Professor of Greek in Edinburgh University, who had just translated Goethe's *Faust* into the English tongue. 'I went about half an hour ago to call upon a sort of Professor here to whom I had a letter and a *Faust* to present from Blackie—found him ill and confined to bed—was admitted, however, very well received, and shall call again when I think there is a chance of his being better. I have still another Professor to call on with a letter and book from Blackie, and there my acquaintance with the society of Berlin is likely to terminate.' One other introduction to Ferrier on this expedition to Germany is mentioned in a note from his aunt, Miss Susan Ferrier, the only letter to her nephew that has apparently been preserved: whether or not he availed himself of the offer, history does not record. It runs as follows:—

'Edinr., *1st August*.

'I could not get a letter to Lord Corehouse's German sister (Countess Purgstall), as it seems she is in bad health, and not fit to entertain vagabonds; but I enclose a very kind one from my friend, Mrs. Erskine, to the ambassadress at

Munich, and if you don't go there you may send it by post, as it will be welcome at any time on its own account.'

It was, as has been said, only about three years previously to this visit that Hegel had passed away at Berlin, and one wonders whether Ferrier first began to interest himself in his writings at this time, and whether he visited the graveyard near the city gate where Hegel lies, close to his great predecessor Fichte. One would almost think this last was so from the exact description given in his short biography of Hegel; and it is significant that on his return he brought with him a medallion and a photograph of the great philosopher. This would seem to indicate that his thoughts were already tending in the direction of Hegelian metaphysics, but how far this was so we cannot tell. Certainly the knowledge of the German language acquired by Ferrier during this visit to the country proved most valuable to him, and enabled him to study its philosophy at a time when translations were practically non-existent, and few had learned to read it. That knowledge must indeed have been tolerably complete, for in 1851, when Sir Edward Bulwer (afterwards Lord Lytton) was about to republish his translation of Schiller's Ballads, he corresponded with Ferrier regarding the accuracy and exactness of his work. He afterwards, in the preface to the volume, acknowledges the great services Ferrier had rendered; and in dedicating the book to him, speaks of the debt of gratitude he owes to one whose 'critical judgment and skill in detecting the finer shades of meaning in the original' had been so useful. Ferrier likewise has the credit, accorded him by De Quincey, of having corrected several errors in *all* the English translations of *Faust* then extant—errors which were not merely literary inaccuracies, but which also detracted from the vital sense of the original. As to Lord Lytton, Ferrier must at this time have been interested in his writings; for in a letter to Miss Wilson, he advises her to read Bulwer's *Pilgrims of the Rhine* if she wishes for a description of the scenery, and speaks of the high esteem with which he was regarded by the Germans.

It was in 1837 that Ferrier married the young lady with whom he had so long corresponded. The marriage was in all respects a happy one. Mrs. Ferrier's gifts and graces, inherited from her father, will not soon be forgotten, either in St. Andrews where she lived so long, or in Edinburgh, the later home of her widowhood. One whose spirits were less gay might have found a husband whose interests were so completely in his work—and that a work in which she could not share—difficult to deal with; but she possessed understanding to appreciate that work, as well as humour, and could accommodate herself to the circumstances in which she found herself; while he, on his part, entered into the gaiety on occasion with the best. A friend and student of the St. Andrews' days writes of Ferrier: 'He married his cousin Margaret, Professor's Wilson's daughter, and I don't doubt that a shorthand report of their courtship would have been better worth reading than nine hundred and ninety-nine out of every thousand courtships, for she had wit as well as beauty, and he was capable of appreciating both. No more charming woman have I ever seen or heard making game of mankind in general, and in particular of pedants and hypocrites. She would even laugh at her husband on occasion, but it was dangerous for any volunteer to try to help her in that sport. A finer-looking couple I have never seen.[5]

During her infancy Edinburgh had become Mrs. Ferrier's home, though she made frequent visits to Westmorland, of whose dialect she had a complete command. The courtship, however, had been for the most part carried on at the picturesque old house of Gorton, where 'Christopher North' was temporarily residing, and which, situated as it is overlooking the lovely glen made immortal by the name of Hawthornden, in view of Roslin Chapel, and surrounded by old-fashioned walks and gardens, must have been an ideal spot for a romantic couple like the Ferriers to roam in. Another friend writes of Wilson's later home at Elleray: 'In his hospitable house, where the wits of *Blackwood* gathered at intervals and visited individually in season and out of season, his daughter saw strange men of genius, such as few young ladies had the fortune to see, and heard talk such as hardly another has the fortune to hear. Lockhart, with his caricatures and his incisive sarcasm, was an intimate of the house. The Ettrick Shepherd, with his plaid and homely Doric, broke in occasionally, as did also De Quincey, generally towards midnight, when he used to sit pouring forth his finely-balanced, graceful sentences far on among the small hours of the morning. There were students, too, year after year, many of them not undistinguished, and some of whom had, we doubt not, ideas of their own regarding the flashing hazel eyes of their eloquent Professor's eldest daughter.' But her cousin was her choice, though wealth offered no attraction, and neither side had reason to regret the marriage of affection.

At the time of his marriage Ferrier had been practising at the Bar, probably with no great measure of success, seeing that his heart was not really set upon his work. It was at this period that he first began to write, and his first contribution to literature took the form of certain papers contributed to *Blackwood's Magazine*, the subject being the 'Philosophy of Consciousness.' From that time onwards Ferrier continued to write on philosophic or literary topics until his death, and many of these writings were first published in the famous magazine.

Before entering, however, on any consideration of Ferrier's writings and of the philosophy of the day, it might be worth while to try to picture to ourselves the social conditions and feelings of the time, in order that we may get some idea of the influences which surrounded him, and be assisted in our efforts to understand his outlook.

In the beginning of the nineteenth century Scotland had been ground down by a strange tyranny—the tyranny of one man as it seemed, which man was Henry Dundas, first Viscount Melville, who for many long years ruled our country as few countries have been ruled before. What this despotism meant it is difficult for us, a century later, to figure to ourselves. All offices were dependent on his patronage; it was to him that everyone had to look for whatever post, advancement, or concession was required. And Dundas, with consummate power and administrative ability, moulded Scotland to his will, and by his own acts made her what she was before the world. But all the while, though unperceived, a new spirit was really dawning; the principles of the Revolution, in spite of everything, had spread, and all unobserved the time-spirit made its influence felt below a surface of apparent calm. It laid hold first of all of the common people—weavers and the like: it roused these rough, uneducated men to a sense of wrong and the resolution to seek a remedy. Not much, however, was accomplished. Some futile risings took place—risings pitiable in their inadequacy—of hard-working weavers armed with pikes and antiquated muskets. Of course, such rebels were easily suppressed; the leaders were sentenced to execution or transportation, as the case might be; but though peace apparently was restored and public meetings to oppose the Government were rigorously suppressed, trade and manufactures were arising: Scotland was not really dead, as she appeared. A new life was dawning: reform was in the air, and in due time made its presence felt. But the memory of these times of political oppression, when the franchise was the privilege of the few, and of the few who were entirely out of sympathy with the most part of their countrymen or their country's wants, remained with the people just as did the 'Killing-time' of Covenanting days two centuries before. Time heals the wounds of a country as of an individual, but the operation is slow, and it is doubtful whether either period of history will ever be forgotten. At anyrate, if they are so as this century closes, they were not in the Scotland known to Ferrier; they were still a very present memory and one whose influence was keenly felt.

And along with this political struggle yet another struggle was taking place, no less real though not so evident. The religion of the country had been as dead as was the politics in the century that was gone—dead in the sleep of Moderatism and indifferentism. But it, too, had awakened; the evangelical school arose, liberty of church government was claimed, a liberty which, when denied it, rent the Established Church in twain.

In our country it has been characteristic that great movements have usually begun with those most in touch with its inmost life, the so-called lower orders of its citizens. The nobles and the kings have rather followed than taken the lead. In the awakening of the present century this at anyrate was the case. 'Society,' so called, remained conservative in its view for long after the people had determined to advance. Scott, it must be remembered, was a retrogressive influence. The romanticism of his novels lent a charm to days gone by which might or might not be deserved; but they also encouraged their readers to imagine a revival of those days of chivalry as a possibility even now, when men were crying for their rights, when they had awakened to a sense of their possessions, and would take nothing in their place. The real chieftains were no more; they were imitation chieftains only who were playing at the game, and it was a game the clansmen would not join in. Few exercises could be more strange than first to read the account of Scottish life in one of the immortal novels by Scott dealing with last century, and then to turn to Miss Ferrier or Galt, depicting a period not so very different. Setting aside all questions of genius, where comparison would be absurd, it would seem as if a beautiful enamel had been removed, and a bare reality revealed, somewhat sordid in comparison. The life was not really sordid,—realism as usual had overshot its mark,—but the enamel had been somewhat thickly laid, and might require to be removed, if truth were to be revealed.

So in the higher grades of Edinburgh society the enamel of gentility has done its best to prejudice us against much true and genuine worth. It was characterised by a certain conventional unconventionality, a certain 'preciosity' which brought it near deserving a still stronger name, and it maintained its right to formulate the canons of criticism for the kingdom. Edinburgh, it must be recollected, was no 'mean city,' no ordinary provincial town. It was still esteemed a metropolis. It had its aristocracy, though mainly of the order of those unable to bear the greater expense of London life. It had no manufactories to speak of, no mercantile class to 'vulgarise' it; it possessed a University, and the law courts of the nation. But above all it had a literary society. In the beginning of the century it had such men as Henry Mackenzie, Dugald Stewart, John Playfair, Dr. Gregory, Dr. Thomas Brown, not to speak of Scott and Jeffrey—a society unrivalled out of London. And in later days, when these were gone, others rose to fill their places.

Of course, in addition to the movement of the working people, there was an educated protest against Toryism, and it was made by a party who, to their credit be it said, risked their prospects of advancement for the principles of freedom. In their days Toryism, we must recollect, meant something very different from what it might be supposed to signify in our own. It meant an attitude of obstruction as regards all change from established standards of whatever kind; it signified a point of view which said that grievances should be unredressed unless it was in its interest to redress them. The new party of opposition included in its numbers Whig lawyers like Gibson Craig and Henry Erskine, in earlier days, and Francis Jeffrey and Lord Cockburn later on; a party of progress was also formed within the Church, and the same within the precincts of the University. The movement, as became a movement on the political side largely headed by lawyers, had no tendency to violence; it was moderate in its policy, and by no means revolutionary—indeed it may be doubted whether there ever was much tendency to revolt even amongst those working men who expressed themselves most strongly. The advance party, however, carried the day, and when Ferrier began to write, Scotland was in a very different state from that of twenty years before. The Reform Bill had passed, and men had the moulding of their country's destiny practically placed within their hands. In the University, again, Sir William Hamilton, a Whig, had just been appointed to the Chair of Logic, while Moncreiff, Chalmers, and the rest, were prominent in the Church. The traditions of literary Edinburgh at the beginning of the century had been kept up by a circle amongst whom Lockhart, Wilson, and De Quincey may be mentioned; now Carlyle, who had left Edinburgh not long before, was coming into notice, and a new era seemed to be dawning, not so glorious as the past, but more untrammelled and more free.

How philosophy was affected by the change, and how Ferrier assisted in its progress, it is our business now to tell; but we must first briefly sketch the history of Scottish speculation to this date, in order to show the position in which he found it.

CHAPTER III

PHILOSOPHY BEFORE FERRIER'S DAY

In attempting to give some idea of philosophy as it was in Scotland in the earlier portion of the present century, we shall have to go back two hundred years or thereabout, in order to find a satisfactory basis from which to start. For philosophy, as no one realised more than Ferrier, is no arbitrary succession of systems following one upon another as their propounders might decree; it is a development in the truest and highest significance of that word. It means the gradual working out of the questions which reason sets to be answered; and though it seems as if we had sometimes to turn our faces backwards, and to revert to systems of bygone days, we always find, when we look more closely, that in our onward course we have merely dropped some thread in our web, the recovery of which is requisite in order that it may be duly taken up and woven with the rest.

At the time of which we write the so-called 'Scottish School' of Reid, Stewart, and Beattie reigned supreme in orthodox Scotland; it had undisputed power in the Universities, and besides this obtained a very reputable place in the estimation of Europe, and more especially of France. As it was this school more especially that Ferrier spent much of his time in combating, it is its history and place that we wish shortly to describe. To do so, however, it is needful to go back to its real founder, Locke, in order that its point of view may fairly be set forth.

In applying his mind to the views of Locke, the ordinary man finds himself arriving at very commonplace and well-accustomed conceptions. Locke, indeed, may reasonably be said to represent the ideas of common, everyday life. The ordinary man does not question the reality of things, he accepts it without asking any questions, and bases his theories—scientific or otherwise—upon this implied reality. Locke worked out the theory which had been propounded by Lord Bacon, that knowledge is obtained by the observation of facts which are implicitly accepted as realities; and what, it was asked, could be more self-evident and sane? It is easy to conceive a number of perceiving minds upon the one hand, ready to take up perceptions of an outside material substance upon the other. The mind may be considered as a piece of white paper—a *tabula rasa*, as it was called—on which external things may make what impression they will, and knowledge is apparently explained at once. But though Locke certainly succeeded in making these terms the common coin of ordinary life, difficulties crop up when we come to examine them more closely. After all, it is evident, the only knowledge our mind can have is a knowledge of its own ideas—ideas which are, of course, caused by something which is outside, or at least, as Locke would say, by its *quality*. Now, from this it would appear that these 'ideas' after all come between the mind and the 'thing,' whatever it is, that causes them—that is to say, we can perhaps maintain that we only know our 'ideas,' and not things as in themselves. Locke passes into elaborate distinctions between primary qualities of things, of which he holds exact representations are given, and secondary qualities, which are not in the same position; but the whole difficulty we meet with is summed up in the question whether we really *know* substance, or whether it is that we can only hope to know ideas, and 'suppose' some substratum of reality outside. Then another difficulty is that we can hardly really know our *selves*. How can we know that the self exists; and if, like Malebranche, we speak of God revealing substance to us, how do we know about God? We cannot form any 'general' impressions, have any 'general' knowledge; only a sort of conglomeration of unrelated or detached bits of knowledge can possibly come home to us. The fact is, that modern philosophy starts with two separate and self-existent substances; that it does not see how they can be combined, and that the 'white-paper' theory is so abstract that we can never arrive at self-consciousness by its means.

Berkeley followed out the logical consequences of Locke, though perhaps he hardly knew where these would carry him. He acknowledged that we know nothing but ideas—nothing outside of our mind. But he adds the conception of self, and by analogy the conception of God, who acts as a principle of causation. Whether there is necessary connection in his sensations or not, he does not say. Hume followed with criticism, scathing and merciless. He states that all we know of is the experience we have; and by experience he signifies perceptions. Ideas to him are nothing more than perceptions, and whether they are ideas simply of the mind, or ideas of some object, is to him the same. If we begin to imagine such conceptions as those of universality or necessity, of God or the self, beyond a complex of successive ideas, we are going farther than experience permits. We cannot connect our perceptions with an object, nor can we get beyond what experience allows. Custom merely brings about certain conclusions which are often enough misleading. It connects effect and cause, really different events: it brings about ideas of morality very often deceptive. We have our custom of regarding things, another has his—who can say which is correct? All we can do is, what seems a hopeless task enough—we can try to show how these unrelated particulars seem by repetition to produce an illusionary connection in our minds.

Both mind and matter appear, then, to be wanting, and experience alone is suggested as the means of solving the difficulty in which we are placed—a point in the argument which left an opportunity open to Kant to suggest a new development, to ask whether things being found inadequate in producing knowledge, we might not ask if knowledge could not be more successful with things. But it is the Scottish lines of attempted solution that we wish to follow out, and not the German. Perhaps they are not so very different.

Philosophy, as Reid found it, was in a bad way enough, as far as the orthodox mind of Scotland was concerned. All justification for belief in God, in immortality, in all that was held sacred in a century of much orthodoxy if little zeal, was gone. Such things might be believed in by those who found any comfort in so believing, but to the educated man who had seriously reflected on them, they were anachronisms. The very desperateness of the case, however, seemed to promise a remedy. Men could not rest in a state of permanent scepticism, in a world utterly incapable of being rationally explained. Even the propounder of the theories allowed this to be true; and as for others, they felt that they were rational beings, and this signified that there was system in the world.

A champion arose when things were at their worst in Thomas Reid, the founder, or at least the chiefest ornament, of the so-called Scottish School of Philosophy. He it was who set himself to add the principle of the coherence of the Universe, and the consequent possibility of establishing Faith once more in the world. Reid, to begin with, instead of looking at Hume's results as serious, regarded them as necessarily absurd. He started a new theory of his own, the theory of Immediate Perception, which signified that we are able immediately to apprehend—not ideas only, but the Truth. And how, we may ask, can this be done?

It had been pointed out first of all that sensations as understood by Locke— that is, the relations so called by Locke—might be separated from sensation in itself; in fact, that these first pertained to mind. Hence we have a dualistic system given us to start with, and the question is how the two sides are to be connected? What does this theory of Immediate Perception, which Reid puts forward as the solution, mean? Is it just a mechanical union of two antitheses, or is it something more?

As to this last, perhaps the real answer would be that it both is, and is not. That is, the philosophy of Reid would seem still dualistic in its nature; it certainly implies the mechanical contact of two confronting substances whose independence is vigorously maintained, in opposition to the idealistic system which it superseded; but in reference to Reid we must recollect that his theory of Immediate Perception was also something more. As regards sensation, for example, he says that we do not begin with unrelated sensations, but with judgment—that is, we refer our sensations to a permanent subject, 'I.' Sensations 'suggest' the nature of a mind and the belief in its existence. And this signifies that we have the power of making inferences—how we do not exactly know, but we believe it to be, not by any special reasoning process, but by the 'common-sense' innately born within us. Common-sense is responsible for a good deal more—for the conceptions of existence and of cause, for instance; for Reid acknowledges that sensations alone must fail to account for ideas such as those of extension, space, and motion. This standpoint seems indeed as if it did not differ widely from the Kantian, but at the same time Reid appears to think that it is not an essential that feelings should be perceptively referred to an external object; the first part of the process of perception is carried on without our consciousness—the mental sensation merely follows—and sensation simply supposes a sentient being and a certain manner in which that being is affected, which leaves us much where we were, as far as the subjectivity of our ideas is concerned. He does not hold that all sensation is a percept involving extension and much else—involving, indeed, existence.

Following upon Reid, Dugald Stewart obtained a very considerable reputation, and he was living and writing at the time Ferrier was a young man. His main idea would, however, seem to have been to guard his utterances carefully, and enter upon no keen discussions or contentions: when a bold assertion is made, it is always under shelter of some good authority. But his rounded phrases gained him considerable admiration, as such writing often does. He carried—perhaps inadvertently—Reid's views farther than he would probably have held as justifiable. He says we are not, properly speaking, conscious of self or the existence of self, but merely of a sensation or some other quality, which, by a *subsequent suggestion* of the understanding, leads to a belief in that which exercises the quality. This is the doctrine of Reid put very crudely, and in a manner calculated to bring us back to unrelated sensation in earnest. Stewart adopted a new expression for Reid's 'common-sense,' *i.e.* the 'fundamental laws of belief,' which might be less ambiguous, but never took popular hold as did the first.

There were many others belonging to this school besides Reid and Stewart, whom it would be impossible to speak of here. The Scottish Philosophy had its work to do, and no doubt understood that work—the first essential in a criticism: it endeavoured to vindicate perception as against sensational idealism, and it only partially succeeded in its task. But we must be careful not to forget that it opened up the way for a more comprehensive and satisfactory point of view. It was with Kant that the distinction arose between sensation and the forms necessary to its perception, the form of space and time, and so on. As to this part of the theory of knowledge, Reid and his school were not clear; they only made an effort to express the fact that something was required to verify our knowledge, but they were far from satisfactorily attaining to their goal. The very name of 'common-sense' was misleading—making people imagine, as it did, that there was nothing in philosophy after all that the man in the street could not know by applying the smallest modicum of reflection to the subject. Philosophy thus came to be considered as superfluous, and it was thought that the sooner we got rid of it and were content to observe the mandates of our hearts, the better for all concerned.

What, then, was the work which Ferrier placed before himself when he commenced to write upon and teach philosophy? He was thoroughly and entirely dissatisfied with the old point of view, the point of view of the 'common-sense' school of metaphysicians, to begin with. Sometimes it seems as though we could not judge a system altogether from the best exponent of it, although theoretically we are always bound to turn to him. In a national philosophy, at least, we want something that will wear, that will bear to be put in ordinary language, something which can be understood of the people, which can be assimilated with the popular religion and politics—in fact, which can really be *lived* as well as thought; and it is only after many years of use that we can really tell whether these conditions have been fulfilled. For this reason we are in some measure justified in taking the popular estimate of a system, and in considering its practical results as well as the value of its theory. Now, the commonly accepted view of the eighteenth-century philosophers in Scotland is that there is nothing very wonderful about the subject—like the *Bourgeois Gentilhomme* of Molière, we are shown that we have been philosophising all our lives, only we never knew it. 'Common-sense'—an attribute with which we all believe we are in some small measure endowed—explains everything if we simply exercise it, and that is open to us all: there has been much talk, it would seem, about nothing; secrets hidden to wise men are revealed to babes, and we have but to keep our minds open in order to receive them.

We are all acquainted with this talk in speculative regions of knowledge, but we most of us also know how disastrous it is to any true advancement in such directions. What happens now is just what happened in the eighteenth century. Men relapse into a self-satisfied indolence of mind: in religion they are content with believing in a sort of general divine Beneficence which will somehow make matters straight, however crooked they may seem to be; and in philosophy they are guided by their instincts, which teach them that what they wish to believe is true.

Now, all this is what Ferrier and the modern movement, largely influenced by German modes of thought, wish to protest against with all their might. The scepticism of Hume and Gibbon was logical, if utterly impossible as a working creed and necessarily ending in absurdity; but this irrational kind of optimism was altogether repugnant to those who demanded a reasonable explanation of themselves and of their place in nature. The question had become summed up in one of superlative importance, namely, the distinction that existed between the natural and supernatural sides of our existence. The materialistic school had practically done away with the latter in its entirety, had said that nature is capable of being explained by mechanical means, and that these must necessarily suffice for us. But the orthodox section adopted other lines; it accepted all the ordinarily received ideas of God, immortality, and the like, but it maintained the existence of an Absolute which can only be inferred, but not presented to the mind, and, strangest of all, declared that the 'last and highest consecration of all true religion must be an altar "To the unknown and unknowable God."'[6] This so-called 'pious' philosophy declares that 'To think that God is, as we can think Him to be, is blasphemy,' and 'A God understood would be no God at all.' The German philosophy saw that if once we are to renounce our reason, or trust to it only within a certain sphere, all hope for us is lost, as far as withstanding the attack of outside enemies is concerned. We are liable to sceptical attacks from every side, and all we can maintain against them is a personal conviction which is not proof. How, then, was the difficulty met?

Kant, as we have said, made an important development upon the position of Hume. Hume had arrived at the point of declaring the particular mind and matter equally incompetent to afford an ultimate explanation of things, and he suggested experience in their place. This is the first note of the new philosophy: experience, not a process of the interaction of two separate things, mind on the one hand, matter on the other, but something comprehending both. This, however, was scarcely realised either by Hume or Kant, though the latter came very near the formulation of it. Kant saw, at least, that things could not produce knowledge, and he therefore changed his front and suggested starting with the knowledge that was before regarded as result—a change in point of view that caused a revolution in thought similar to that caused in our ideas of the natural world by the introduction of the system of Copernicus. Still, while following out his Copernican theory, Kant did not go far enough. His methods were still somewhat psychological in nature. He still regarded thought as something which can be separated from the thinker; he still maintained the existence of things in themselves independent and outside of thought. He gives us a 'theory' of knowledge, when what we want to reach is knowledge itself, and not a subjective conception of it.

Here it is that the Absolute Idealism comes in—the Idealism most associated with the name of Hegel. Hegel takes experience, knowledge, or thought, in another and much more comprehensive fashion than did his predecessors. Knowledge, in fact, is all-comprehending; it embraces both sides in itself, and explains them as 'moments,' *i.e.* complementary factors in the one Reality. To make this clearer: we have been all along taking knowledge as a dualistic process, as having two sides involved in it, a subject and an object. Now, Hegel says our mistake is this: we cannot make a separation of such a kind except by a process of abstraction: the one really implies the other, and could not possibly exist without it. We may in our ordinary pursuits do so, without doubt; we may concentrate our attention on one side or the other, as the case may be; we may look at the world as if it could be explained by mechanical means, as, indeed, to a certain point it can. But, Hegel says, these explanations are not sufficient; they can easily be shown to be untrue, when driven far enough: the world is something larger; it has the ideal side as well as the real, and, as we are placed, they are both necessarily there, and must both be recognised, if we are to attain to true conceptions.

Without saying that Ferrier wholly assimilated the modern German view,—for of course he did not,—he was clearly largely influenced by it, more largely perhaps than he was even himself aware. It particularly met the present difficulties with which he was confronted. The negative attitude was felt to be impossible, and the other, the Belief which then, as now, was so strongly advocated, the Belief which meant a more or less blind acceptance of a spiritual power beyond our own, the Belief in the God we cannot know and glory in not being able so to know, he felt to be an equal impossibility. Ferrier, and many others, asked the question, Are these alternatives exhaustive? Can we not have a rational explanation of the world and of ourselves? Can we not, that is, attain to freedom? The new point of view seemed in some measure to meet the difficulty, and therefore it was looked to with hope and anticipation even although its bearing was not at first entirely comprehended. Ferrier was one of those who perceived the momentous consequences which such a change of front would cause, and he set himself to work it out as best he could. In an interesting paper which he writes on 'The Philosophy of Common-Sense,' with special reference to Sir William Hamilton's edition of the works of Dr. Reid, we see in what way his opinions had developed.

The point which Ferrier made the real crux of the whole question of philosophy was the distinction which exists between the ordinary psychological doctrine of perception and the metaphysical. The former drew a distinction between the perceiving mind and matter, and based its reasonings on the assumed modification of our minds brought about by matter regarded as self-existent, *i.e.* existent in itself and without regard to any perceiving mind. Now,

Ferrier points out that this system of 'representationalism,' of representative ideas, necessarily leads to scepticism; for who can tell us more, than that we have certain ideas—that is, how can it be known that the real matter supposed to cause them has any part at all in the process? Scepticism, as we saw before, has the way opened up for it, and it doubts the existence of matter, seeing that it has been given no reasonable grounds for belief in it, while Idealism boldly denies its instrumentality and existence. What then, he asks, of Dr. Reid and his School of Common-Sense? Reid cannot say that matter is known in consciousness, but what he does say is that something innately born within us forces us to believe in its existence. But then, as Ferrier pertinently points out, scepticism and idealism do not merely doubt and deny the existence of a self-existent matter as an object of consciousness, but also because it is no object of belief. And what has Reid to show for his beliefs? Nothing but his word. We must all, Ferrier says, be sceptics or idealists; we are all forced on to deny that matter in any form exists, for it is only self-existent matter that we recognise as psychologists. Stewart tries to reinstate it by an appeal to 'direct observation,' an appeal which, Ferrier truly says, is manifestly absurd; reasoning is useless, and we must, it would appear, allow any efforts we might make towards rectifying our position to be recognised as futile.

But now, Ferrier says, the metaphysical solution of the problem comes in. We are in an *impasse*, it would appear; the analysis of the given fact is found impossible. But the failure of psychology opens up the way to metaphysic. 'The turning-round of thought from psychology to metaphysic is the true interpretation of the Platonic conversion of the soul from ignorance to knowledge, from mere opinion to certainty and satisfaction; in other words, from a discipline in which the thinking is only *apparent*, to a discipline in which the thinking is *real*.' 'The difference is as great between "the science of the human mind" and metaphysic, as it is between the Ptolemaic and the Copernican astronomy, and it is very much of the same kind.' It is not that metaphysic proposes to do *more* than psychology; it aims at nothing but what it can fully overtake, and does not propose to carry a man farther than his tether extends, or the surroundings in which he finds himself. Metaphysic in the hands of all true astronomers of thought, from Plato to Hegel, if it accomplishes more, attempts less.

Metaphysic, Ferrier says, demands the whole given fact, and that fact is summed up in this: 'We apprehend the perception of an object,' and nothing short of this suffices—that is, not the perception of matter, but our apprehension of that perception, or what we before called knowledge, ultimate knowledge in its widest sense. And this given fact is unlike the mere perception of matter, for it is capable of analysis and is not simply subjective and egoistic. Psychology recognises perception on the one hand (subjective), and matter on the other (objective), but metaphysic says the distinction ought to be drawn between 'our apprehension' and 'the perception-of-matter,' the latter being one fact and indivisible, and on no account to be taken as two separate facts or thoughts. The whole point is, that by no possible means can the perception-of-matter be divided into two facts or existences, as was done by psychology. And Ferrier goes on to point out that this is not a subjective idealism, it is not a condition of the human soul alone, but it 'dwells apart, a mighty and independent system, a city fitted up and upheld by the living God.' And in authenticating this last belief Ferrier calls in internal convictions, 'common-sense,' to assist the evidence of speculative reason, where, had he followed more upon the lines of the great German Idealists, he might have done without it.

Now, Ferrier continues, we are safe against the cavils of scepticism; the metaphysical theory of perception steers clear of all the perplexities of representationalism; for it gives us in perception one only object, the perception of matter; the objectivity of this *datum* keeps us clear from subjective idealism.

From the perception of matter, a fact in which man merely participates, Ferrier infers a Divine mind, of which perceptions are the property: they are states of the everlasting intellect. The exercise of the senses is the condition upon which we are permitted to apprehend or participate in the objective perception of material things. This, shortly, is the position from which he starts.

CHAPTER IV

'FIERCE WARRES AND FAITHFUL LOVES'

'If Ferrier's life should be written hereafter,' said one, who knew and valued him, just after his death,[7] 'let his biographer take for its motto these five words from the *Faery Queen* which the biographer of the Napiers has so happily chosen.' Ferrier's life was not, what it perhaps seems, looking back on its comparatively uneventful course, consistently calm and placid,—a life such as is commonly supposed to befit those who soar into lofty speculative heights, and find the 'difficult air' in which they dwell suited to their contemplative temperaments. Ferrier was intrepid and daring in his reasoning; a sort of free lance, Dr. Skelton says he was considered in orthodox philosophical circles; a High Tory in politics, yet one who did not hesitate to probe to the bottom the questions which came before him, even though the task meant changing the whole attitude of mind from which he started. And once sure of his point, Ferrier never hesitated openly to declare it. What he hated most of all was 'laborious dulness and consecrated feebleness'; commonplace orthodoxy was repugnant to him in the extreme, and possibly few things gave him more sincere pleasure than violently to combat it. The fighting instinct is proper to most men who have 'stuff' in them, and Ferrier in spite of his slight and delicately made frame was manly to the core. But, as the same writer says, 'though combative over his books and theories, his nature was singularly pure, affectionate, and tolerant. He loved his friends even better than he hated his foes. His prejudices were invincible; but, apart from his prejudices, his mind was open and receptive— prepared to welcome truth from whatever quarter it came.' Such a keen, eager nature was sure to be in the fray if battle had to be fought, and we think none the worse of him for that. Battles of intellect are not less keen than battles of physical strength, and much more daring and subtlety may be called into play in the fighting of them; and Ferrier, refined, sensitive, fastidious, as he was, had his battles to fight, and fought them with an eagerness and zeal almost too great for the object he had in view.

After his marriage in 1837, Ferrier devoted his attention almost entirely to the philosophy he loved so well. He did not succeed—did not perhaps try to succeed—at the Bar, to which he had been called. Many qualities are required by a successful advocate besides the subtle mind and acute reasoning powers which Ferrier undoubtedly possessed: possibly—we might almost say probably—these could have been cultivated had he made the effort. He had, to begin with, a fair junior counsel's practice, owing to his family connections, and this might have been easily developed; his ambition, however, did not soar in the direction of the law courts, and he did not give that whole-hearted devotion to the subject which is requisite if success is to follow the efforts of the novice. But if he was not attracted by the work at the Parliament House, he was attracted elsewhere; and to his first mistress, Philosophy, none could be more faithful. In other lines, it is true, he read much and deeply: literature in its widest sense attracted him as it would attract any educated man. Poetry, above all, he loved, in spite of the tale sometimes told against him, that he gravely proposed turning *In Memoriam* into prose in order to ascertain logically 'whether its merits were sustained by reason as well as by rhyme'—a proposition which is said greatly to have entertained its author, when related to him by a mutual friend. Works of imagination he delighted in—all spheres of literature appealed to him; he had the sense of form which is denied to many of his craft; he wrote in a style at once brilliant and clear, and carelessness on this score in some of the writings of his countrymen irritated him, as those sensitive to such things are irritated. He has often been spoken of as a living protest against the materialism of the age, working away in the quiet, regardless of the busy throng, without its ambitions and its cares. Sometimes, of course, he temporarily deserted the work he loved the best for regions less remote; sometimes he consented to lecture on purely literary topics, and often he wrote biographies for a dictionary, or articles or reviews for *Blackwood's Edinburgh Magazine*. As it was to this serial that Ferrier made his most important contributions, both philosophic and literary, for the next fifteen years, and as it was in its pages that the development of his system may be traced, a few words about its history may not be out of place, although it is a history with which we have every reason to be familiar now.

About 1816 the *Edinburgh Review* reigned supreme in literature. What was most strange, however, was that the Conservative party, so strong in politics, had no literary organ of their own—and this at a time when the line of demarcation between the rival sides in politics was so fixed that no virtue could be recognised in an opponent or in an opponent's views, even though they were held regarding matters quite remote from politics. The Whig party, though in a minority politically and socially, represented a minority of tremendous power, and possessed latent capabilities which soon broke forth into action. At this time, for instance, they had literary ability of a singularly marked description; they were not bound down by traditions as were their opponents, and were consequently much more free to strike out lines of their own, always of course under the guidance of that past-master in criticism, Francis Jeffrey. Although his words were received as oracular by his friends, this dictatorship in matters of literary taste was naturally extremely distasteful to those who differed from him, especially as the influence it exerted was not a local or national influence alone, but one which affected the opinion of the whole United Kingdom. For a time, no doubt, the party was so strong that the matter was not taken as serious, but it soon became evident that a strenuous effort must be made if affairs were to be placed on a better footing, and if a protest were to be raised against the cynical criticism in which the Reviewers indulged. Consequently, in April 1817, a literary periodical called the *Edinburgh Monthly Magazine* was started by two gentlemen of some experience in literary matters, with the assistance of Mr. William Blackwood, an enterprising Edinburgh publisher, whose reputation had grown of recent years to considerable dimensions. This magazine was not a great success: the editors and publisher did not agree, and finally Mr. Blackwood purchased the formers' share in it, took over the magazine himself, and, to make matters clear, gave it his name; thus in October of the same year the first number of *Blackwood's Edinburgh Magazine* appeared. From a quiet and unobtrusive 'Miscellany' the magazine developed into a strongly partisan periodical, with a brilliant array of young contributors, determined to oppose the *Edinburgh Review* régime with all its might, and not afraid to speak its mind respecting the literary gods of the day. Every month some one came under the lash; Coleridge, Leigh Hunt, and many others were dealt with in terms unmeasured in their severity, and in the very first number appeared the famous 'Chaldee Manuscript' which made the hair of Edinburgh society stand on end with horror. In spite of the immoderate expression of its opinions, the magazine flourished—it was fresh and novel, and much genius was enlisted in writing for its pages. The editor's identity was always matter for conjecture; but though the contributors included a number of distinguished men, such as Mackenzie, De Quincey, Hogg, Fraser Tytler, and Jameson, there were two names which were always associated with the periodical—those of John Gibson Lockhart and Ferrier's uncle and father-in-law, John Wilson. The latter in particular was often held to be the real editor whom everyone was so anxious to discover, but this belief has been emphatically denied. Although the management might appear to be in the control of a triumvirate, Blackwood himself kept the supreme power in his hands, whatever he might at times find it politic to lead outsiders to infer.

When Ferrier began to write for it in 1838, *Blackwood's Magazine* was not of course the same fiery publication of twenty years before; nor were Ferrier's articles for the most part of a nature such as to appeal strongly to an excitable and partisan public. Things had changed much since 1817: the Reform Bill had passed; the politics of the country were very different; the Toryism of Ferrier and his friends was quite unlike the Toryism of the early part of the century: it more resembled the Conservatism or Traditionalism of a yet later date, which objected to violent changes only owing to their violence, and by no means to reform, if gradually carried out. This policy was reflected in *Maga's* pages, to which Ferrier would naturally turn when he wished to reach the public ear, both from family association and hereditary politics. His first contribution was certainly not light in character; nor did it resemble the 'bright, racy' articles which are supposed to be the requisite for modern serial publications. The subject was 'An Introduction to the Philosophy of Consciousness,' and it consisted of a series of papers contributed during two successive years (1838 and 1839), which really embodied the result of the work in which Ferrier had during the past few years been engaged, and signified a complete divergence from the accepted manner of regarding consciousness, and a protest against the 'faith-philosophy' which it became Ferrier's special mission to combat. Perhaps it is only in Scotland that a public could be found sufficiently interested in speculative questions to make them the subject of interest to a fairly wide and general circle, such as would be likely to peruse the pages of a monthly magazine like Blackwood's. But of this interesting contribution to metaphysical speculation, in which Ferrier commenced his philosophical career by grappling with the deepest and most fundamental questions in a manner, as Hamilton acknowledges, hitherto unattempted in the humbler speculations of this country, we shall speak later on, as also of his further contributions to the magazine.

In the year 1821, Sir William Hamilton had been a candidate for the Chair of Moral Philosophy along with John Wilson, Ferrier's future father-in-law. In spite of Wilson's literary gifts, there is probably no question that of the two his opponent was best qualified to teach the subject, owing to the greatness of his philosophical attainments and the profundity of his learning. But in the temper of the time the merits of the candidates could not be calmly weighed by the Town Council, the electing body; and Hamilton was a Whig, and a Whig contributor to that atheistical and Jacobin *Edinburgh Review*, and was therefore on no account to be elected. The disappointment to Hamilton was great; but it was slightly salved by his subsequent election—to their credit be it said, for Whig principles were far from popular among them—by the Faculty of Advocates to a chair rendered vacant in 1821 by the resignation of Professor Fraser Tytler—the Chair of Civil History. In 1836, however, Sir William's merits at length received their reward, and he became the Professor of Logic and Metaphysics. When Ferrier probably felt the need of some more lucrative form of employment, he applied for the Chair of History once occupied by Hamilton, and rendered vacant by the resignation of Professor Skene; he obtained the appointment in 1842, and held it for four years subsequently. Large remuneration it certainly did not bring with it, but the duties were comparatively and correspondingly light.[8] Indeed, as attendance was not required of students studying for the degrees in Arts, or for any of the professions, the difficulty was to form a regular class at all. The salary paid to Sir William was £100 a year, and even this small sum was apparently only to be obtained with difficulty. The main advantage of holding the chair at all was the prospect it held out of succeeding later on to some more important office. Of Ferrier's class-work at this time we know but little. The reading requisite for the post was likely to prove useful in later days, and could not have been uncongenial; but probably in a class sometimes formed—if tradition speak aright—of one solitary student, the work of preparation would not be taken very seriously. Anyhow, there was plenty of time left to pursue his philosophic studies; and in 1844-45, when Sir William Hamilton came so near to death, Ferrier acted as his substitute, and carried on his classes with zeal and with success—a success which was warmly acknowledged by the Professor. Of course, though he conducted the examinations and other class-work, Ferrier merely read the lectures written by Hamilton; else there might, one would fancy, be found to be a lack of continuity between the deliverances of the two staunch friends but uncompromising opponents. Any differences of opinion made, however, no difference in their friendship. The distress of Ferrier on his friend's sudden paralytic seizure has already been described; to his affectionate nature it was no small thing that one for whom he had so deep a regard came so very near death's door. Every Sunday while in Edinburgh, he spent the afternoon in walking with his friend and in talking of the subjects which most interested both.

Of these early days Professor Fraser writes:—'My personal intercourse with Ferrier was very infrequent, but very delightful when it did occur. He was surely the most picturesque figure among the Scottish philosophers—easy, graceful, humorous, eminently subtle, and with a fine literary faculty—qualities not conspicuous in most of them. When I was a private member of Sir W. Hamilton's advanced class in metaphysics in 1838-39, and for some years after, I was often at Sir William's house, and Ferrier was sometimes of the party on these occasions. I remember his kindly familiarity with us students, the interest and sympathy with which he entered into metaphysical discussion, his help and co-operation in a metaphysical society which we were endeavouring to organise. His essays on the Philosophy of Consciousness were then being issued in *Blackwood*, and were felt to open questions strange at a time when speculation was almost dead in Scotland—Reid at a discount, Brown found empty, and Hamilton, with Kant, only struggling into ascendency.

'In these days, if I remember right, Ferrier lived in Carlton Street, Stockbridge—an advocate whose interest was all in letters and philosophy, a student of simple habits, fond of German, not a conspicuous talker, of easy polished manners and fond of a joke, with a scientific interest in all sorts of facts and their meanings, and perhaps a disposition to paradox. I remember the interest he took in phenomena of "mesmeric sleep," as it was called. An eminent student was sometimes induced for experiment to submit himself to mesmeric influence at these now far-off evening gatherings at Sir William's. To Ferrier the phenomena suggested curious speculation, but I think without scientific result.' The subject was one on which Ferrier afterwards wrote in *Blackwood*, and it was a subject which always had the deepest interest for him. It, however, as he believed, cost him the friendship of Professor Cairns, a frequent subject at these informal séances, and one whom Ferrier rashly twitted for what he evidently regarded as a weakness, his easily accomplished subjection to the application of mesmeric power.

In 1845 the Chair of Moral Philosophy in the University of St. Andrews, then occupied by Dr. Cook, and once held by Dr. Chalmers, became vacant by the former's death, and Ferrier entered as a candidate. Highly recommended as he was by Hamilton and others, Ferrier was the successful applicant, and St. Andrews became his home for nineteen years thereafter, or until his death in 1864.

Such is a bald statement of the facts of what would seem a singularly uneventful life. Life divided between the study, library, and classroom, there was little room for incident outside the ordinary incidents of domestic and academic routine. Yet Ferrier never sank into the conventionality which life in a small University town might induce. His interests were always fresh; he was constantly engaged in writing and rewriting his lectures, which, unlike some of his calling, he was not content to read and re-read from year to year unaltered. His thoughts were constantly on his subject and on his students, planning how best to communicate to them the knowledge that he was endeavouring to convey—a life which came as near the ideal of philosophic devotion as is perhaps possible in this nineteenth century of turmoil and unrest. Still, gentleman and man of culture as he was, Ferrier had a fighting side as well, and that side was once or twice aroused in all the vehemence of its native strength.

Twice Ferrier made application for a philosophical chair in the town of his birth and boyhood. In 1852, when his father-in-law, John Wilson, retired, he became a candidate for the professorship of Moral Philosophy in the University of Edinburgh; and then again, in 1856, he offered himself as a successor to Sir William Hamilton as Professor of Logic and Metaphysics. On neither occasion was he successful, and on both occasions he suffered much from calumnious statements respecting his 'German' and unorthodox views—a kind of calumny which is more than likely to arise and carry weight when the judges are men of honourable character but of little education, men to whom a shibboleth is everything and real progress in learning nothing. On the first occasion there were several candidates who submitted their applications, but on Professor M'Cosh's retiring from the combat, the two who were 'in the running' were Professor Ferrier of St. Andrews and Professor Macdougall of the Free Church College in Edinburgh. It is curious, as instancing the strange change which had come over the politics of Scotland since the Reform Act had passed, that the very influences that told in favour of John Wilson in applying for a professorship in 1821 should thirty years later tell as strongly against his son-in-law. In 1852, nine years after the Disruption, so greatly had matters altered, that the Free Church liberal party carried all before it in the Corporation. And although the liberal journals of the earlier date were never tired of maintaining liberty of thought and action, yet when circumstances changed, the liberty appeared in a somewhat different light; and the qualification of being a Whig was added to a considerable number of appointments both in the Church and in the State. Professor Macdougall, Ferrier's opponent, had held his professorship in the Free Church College, lately established for the teaching of theology and preparation of candidates for the ministry. On the establishment of the College, the subject of Moral Philosophy was considered to be one which should be taught elsewhere than in an 'Erastian' University, and accordingly it was thought necessary to institute the chair occupied by Professor Macdougall. In the first instance the class was eminently successful in point of numbers, and the corresponding class in the University proportionately suffered; but as time went on the attendance in the Free Church class dwindled, and it was considered that this chair need not be continued, but that students might be permitted to attend at the University. When Professor Macdougall now offered himself as candidate for the University chair, there was of course an immediate outcry of a 'job.' Rightly or wrongly it was said, 'Let the Free Church have a Professor of her own body and opinions if she will, but why force him upon the Established Church as well; are her country and ministers to be indoctrinated with Voluntary principles?' There might not have been much force in the argument had the status of the two candidates been the same, but it was evident to all unprejudiced observers that this was far from being the case. And it could hardly be pleaded in justification of the Council's action that they formed their judgment upon the testimonials laid before them; for Ferrier's far exceeded his rival's in weight, if not in strength of expression, and included in their number communications from such men as Sir William Hamilton, De Quincey, Bulwer, Alison, and Lockhart—men the most distinguished of the age. De Quincey's opinion of Ferrier is worth quoting. He says that he regards him as 'the metaphysician of greatest promise among his contemporaries either in England or in Scotland,' and the testimonial which at this time he accorded Ferrier is as remarkable a document as is often produced on such occasions, when commonplace would usually appear to be the object aimed at. It is several pages in length, and goes fully into the question not only of what Ferrier was, but also of what a candidate ought to be. De Quincey speaks warmly of Ferrier's services in respect of the English rendering of *Faust* before alluded to, and points out the benefit there is in having had an education which has run along two separate paths—paths differing from one another in nature, doubtless, but integrating likewise—the one being that resulting from his intercourse with Wilson and his literary coterie, the other that of the course of study he had pursued on German lines. He sums up Ferrier's philosophic qualities by saying, 'Out of Germany, and comparing him with the men of his own generation, such at least as I had any means of estimating, Mr. Ferrier was the only man who exhibited much of true metaphysical subtlety, as contrasted with mere dialectical acuteness.' For this testimonial, we may incidentally mention, Ferrier writes a most interesting letter of thanks, which is published in his *Remains*. As a return for the kindness done him, he 'sets forth a slight chart of the speculative latitudes' he had reached, and which he 'expects to navigate without being wrecked'—really an admirably clear epitome in so short a space of the argument of the *Institutes*.

But to come back to the contest: in spite of testimonials, the fact remained that Ferrier had studied German philosophy, and might have imbibed some German infidelity, while his opponent made no professions of being acquainted either with the German philosophy or language, besides having the advantage of being a Liberal and Free Churchman; and he was consequently appointed to the chair. Of course, there was an outcry. The election was put forward as an argument against the abolition of Tests, though in this case Ferrier, as an Episcopalian, might be said to be a Dissenter equally with his opponent. It was argued that the election should be set aside unless the necessary subscription were made before the Presbytery of the bounds. For a century back such tests had not been exacted as far as the Moral Philosophy chair was concerned, nor would they probably have been so had Ferrier himself been nominated. But though the Presbytery concerned was in this case prepared to go all lengths, it appeared that it was not in its members that the initiative was vested, the practice being to take the oath before the Lord Provost or other authorised magistrate. Consequently, indignant at discovering their impotence, the members of the body retaliated by declaring that they would divert past the new Professor's class the students who should afterwards come within their jurisdiction, and thus, by their foolish action, they probably did their best to bring about the result they deprecated so much—the abolition of Tests in their entirety.

Ecclesiastical feeling ran high at the time, and things were said and done on both sides which were far from being wise or prudent. But the effect on a sensitive nature like Ferrier's is easy to imagine. This was the first blow he had met with, and being the first he did not take it quite so seriously to heart. But when it was followed years later by yet another repulse, signifying to his view an attitude of mind in orthodox Scotland opposed to any liberty of thought amongst its teachers, Ferrier felt the day for silence was ended, and, wisely or unwisely, he published a hot defence of his position in a pamphlet entitled *Scottish Philosophy, the Old and the New*. On this occasion the question had risen above the mere discussion of Church and Tests; the whole future of philosophy in Scotland was, he believed, at stake; it was time, he felt, that someone should speak out his mind, and who more suitable than the leader of the modern movement and the one, as he considered it, who had suffered most by his opinions?

Without having lived through the time or seen something of its effects, it would be difficult to realise how narrow were the bounds allowed to speculative thought some forty years ago in Scotland. Since the old days of Moderatism and apathy there had, indeed, been a great revival of interest in such matters as concerned Belief. Men's convictions were intense and sincere; and what had once been a subject of convention and common usage, had now become the one important topic of their lives. So far the change was all for the good; it promoted many important virtues; it made men serious about serious things; it made them realise their responsibilities as human beings. But as those who lived through it, or saw the results it brought about, must also know, it had another side. A certain spiritual self-assurance sprang into existence, which, though it was bred of intense reality of conviction, brought with it consequences of a specially trying kind to those who did not altogether share in it. As so often happens when a new light dawns, men thought that to them at length *all* truth had been revealed, and acted in accordance with this belief. They formulated their systems—hide-bound almost as before—and decided in their minds that in them they had the standards for judging of their fellows. But Truth is a strange will-o'-the-wisp after all,—when we think we have reached her, she has eluded our grasp,—and so when those rose up who said the end of the matter was not yet, a storm of indignation fell upon their heads. This is what happened with Ferrier and the orthodox Edinburgh world. There might, it was said by the latter, be men lax enough to listen to reasonings such as his, and even to agree with them, but for those who *knew* the truth as it was in its reality, such pandering to latitudinarian doctrines was unpardonable. And as at this time the Town Council of Edinburgh was seriously inclined (some of the members, in the second instance, were the same as those who had adjudicated in the former contest), Ferrier's fate was, he considered, sealed before the question really came before them. Whether the matter was quite as serious as Ferrier thought, it is perhaps unnecessary to say. At anyrate, there was a considerable element of truth in the view he took of it, and he was justified in much—if not in all—of what he said in his defence. The *Institutes*, first published in 1854, had just reached a second edition, so that his views were fairly before the world. What caused the tremendous outburst of opposition we must take another chapter to consider; and then we must try to trace the course of Ferrier's development from the time at which he first began to write on philosophic subjects, and when he openly broke with the Scottish School of Philosophy.

CHAPTER V

DEVELOPMENT OF 'SCOTTISH PHILOSOPHY, THE OLD AND THE NEW'—FERRIER AS A CORRESPONDENT

It is probably in the main a wise rule for defeated candidates to keep silence about the cause of their defeat. But every rule has its exception, and there are times in which we honour a man none the less because—contrary to the dictates of worldly wisdom—he gives voice to the sense of injustice that is rankling in his mind. Ferrier had been disappointed in 1852 in not obtaining the Chair of Moral Philosophy for which he was a candidate; but then he had not published the work which has made his name famous, and his claims were therefore not what afterwards they became. But when in 1856, after the *Institutes* had been two years before the public, and just after the book had reached a second edition, another defeat followed on the first, Ferrier ascribed the result to the opposition to, and misrepresentation of, his system, and claimed with some degree of justice that it was not his merits that were taken into account, but the supposed orthodoxy, or want of orthodoxy, of his views. For this reason he issued a 'Statement' in pamphlet form, entitled *Scottish Philosophy, the Old and the New*, dealing with the matter at length.

In Ferrier's view, a serious crisis had been arrived at in the history of the University of Edinburgh, and one which might lead to yet further evil were not something done to place matters on a better footing. Had the Town Council, the electing body, been affected simply by personal or sectarian feelings, it would not so much have mattered; but when Ferrier was forced to the conclusion that what they did must end in the curtailment of all liberty in regard to philosophical opinion, so far as the University was concerned, he felt the time had come to speak. For a quarter of a century he had devoted the best part of his life and energies to the study of philosophy, and he held he had a duty to discharge to it as one of the public instructors of the land. What cause, he asked, had a body like the Council to say originality was to be proscribed and independence utterly forbidden? Through their liberalism tests had been practically abolished: was another test, far more exacting than the last, to be substituted in their place? A candidate for a philosopher's chair need not be a believer in Christ or a member of the Established Church; but he must, it would appear, believe in Dr. Reid and the Hamiltonian system of philosophy.

The 'common-sense' school, against which Ferrier's attacks were mainly directed, too often found its satisfaction in commonplace statements of obvious facts, and we cannot wonder that Ferrier should ask why Scottish students should be required to pay for 'bottled air' while the whole atmosphere is 'floating with liquid balm that could be had for nothing?'—a question, indeed, which cannot fail to strike whoever tries to wade through certain tedious dissertations of the time, all expressing truths which seem incontrovertible in their nature, but all of which are also inexpressibly uninteresting. Philosophy to Ferrier is not the elementary science that it would appear from these discourses: loose ways of thinking which we ordinarily adopt must, he considers, be rectified and not confirmed. And yet he disclaims the accusation that he has conjured with 'the portentous name of Hegel,' or derived his system from German soil. Hegel, he constantly confesses, is frequently to him inexplicable, and his system is Scottish to the core.

A warm debt of gratitude to Hamilton, Ferrier, it is true, acknowledges even while he differs from his views—a debt to one whose 'soul could travel on eagles' wings,' and from whom he had learned so much—whom, indeed, he had loved so warmly. Hamilton had not agreed with Ferrier; he had thought him wrong, and told him so, and Ferrier was the last to resent this action, or think the less of him for not recanting at his word the conclusions of a lifetime's labour. Provocation, the younger man acknowledges, he had often given him, and 'never was such rough provocation retaliated with such gentle spleen.'

But what most roused Ferrier's ire was, not the criticisms of men like Hamilton, but such as were contained in a pamphlet published by the Rev. Mr. Cairns of Berwick, afterwards Principal Cairns of the United Presbyterian College—a pamphlet which he believed had biassed the judgment of the electors in making their decision. We now know that indirectly they had requested Mr. Cairns's advice, and he, considering that orthodoxy was being seriously threatened by German rationalistic views, had formulated his indictment against Ferrier in the strongest possible terms. He believed that in Ferrier's writings there was an attempt to substitute formal demonstration of real existence for 'belief,' thereby making faith of no effect; also that he denied the separate existence of the material world and the mind, and that (and probably this is the most serious count in the charge) the substantiality of the mind was subverted, and consequently belief in personal identity rendered impossible. He further said that by Ferrier absolute existence is reduced to a mere relation, and finally, that his conception of a Deity is inadequate, and metaphysics and natural theology are divorced.

We cannot, of course, deal in detail with Ferrier's energetic repudiation of the accusation brought so specifically against him. The heat with which he wrote seems scarcely justified now that we look back on it from the standpoint of more than forty years ahead. But we do not realise how much such accusations meant at the time at which they were made—how they affected not a man's personal advancement only, but also the opinion in which he was held by those for whose opinion he cared the most. The greater toleration of the present day may mean corresponding lack of zeal or interest, but surely it also means a recognition of the fact that men may choose their own methods in the search for truth without thereby endangering the object held in view. Mr. Cairns's attack—without intention, for he was an honourable man and able scholar—was unjust. Ferrier does not claim to *prove* existence—he accepts it, and only reasons as to what it is; as to the material world, he acknowledges not a mere material world, but one along with which intelligence is and must be known; the separate existence of mind he likewise denies only in so far as to assert that mind without thought is nonsense. The substantiality of the mind he maintains as the one great permanent existence amid all fluctuations and contingencies, and without personal identity, he tells us, there can be no continued consciousness amid the changes of the unfluctuating existence called the 'I'—though in this regard one feels that something is left to say in criticism, from the orthodox point of view. Absolute existence is indeed reduced into relations, but into relations together constituting the truth, if contradictory in themselves; that is, a concrete, as distinguished from an abstract truth. As to the final accusation of the insufficiency of Ferrier's view of the Deity, it is true he states that the Deity is not independent of His creative powers, revelation and manifestation; but surely this is a worthier conception than the old one of the Unknown God, which tells us to worship we know not what.

The pity is that in this publication, and another on very similar lines,[9] Ferrier allowed himself to turn from philosophical to personal criticism, and to say what he must afterwards have regretted. In the second edition of his first pamphlet these references were modified, and in any case they must be ascribed to the quick temper with which he was naturally endowed, and which led him to express his feelings more strongly than he should, rather than to deliberate judgment. No one was more sensible than he of the danger to which he was subject of allowing himself to be carried off his feet in the heat of argument. This is very clearly shown by a letter to a friend quoted in the *Remains*: 'One thing I would recommend, not to be too sharp in your criticism of others. No one has committed this fault oftener, or is more disposed to commit it than myself; but I am certain that it is not pleasing to the reader, and after an interval it is displeasing to oneself. In the heat and hurry of writing a lecture I often hit a brother philosopher as I think cleverly enough, but on coming to it coolly next year I very seldom repeat the passage.' An admission and acknowledgment which does a proud man like Ferrier credit.

One cannot help speculating on the effect of the mass of criticism and counter-criticism (for there were others who took up the cudgels on either side, once the controversy was fairly started) upon the unfortunate Town Councillors of Edinburgh, to whom they were directed: one would imagine them to wish their powers curtailed if they were to involve their mastering several conflicting theories of existence, and forming a just judgment regarding their respective merits. The exercise of patronage is always a difficult and thankless task, but surely in no case could it have been more difficult than in this, and we can hardly wonder now that the electors simply took the advice of those they deemed most worthy to bestow it; certainly the candidate finally selected was one who did everything in the occupation of his chair to disarm the criticism then brought to bear upon the appointment. In cooler moments probably none would have been readier to admit this than was Ferrier; but when he wrote he was smarting under the sense of having failed to receive a fair consideration of his claims, and he undoubtedly spoke more strongly than the case required.

After this controversy was over, Ferrier's interest in polemical philosophy in great degree waned; and in the quiet of the old University town of St. Andrews—the town which provides so rich a fund of historic interest combined with the academic calm of University life—Ferrier passed the remainder of his days working at his favourite subjects. Sometimes these were varied by incursions into literature, in which his interest grew ever keener; and economics, which was one of the subjects he was bound to teach. His life was uneventful; it was varied little by expeditions into the outer world, much as these would have been appreciated by his friends. His whole interest was centred in his work and in the University in which he taught, and whose well-being was so dear to him. Of his letters, few, unfortunately, have been preserved; and this is the more unfortunate that he had the gift, now comparatively so rare, of expressing himself with ease, and in bright, well-chosen language. Of his correspondents one only seems to have preserved the letters written to him, Mr. George Makgill of Kemback, a neighbouring laird in Fife and advocate in Edinburgh, whose similarity in tastes drew him towards the St. Andrews Philosophy Professor.

Of these letters there are some of sufficient interest to bear quotation. One of the first is written in October 1851 from St. Andrews, and plunges into the deepest topics without much preface. Ferrier says:—

'What is the Beginning of Philosophy? Philosophy must have had the same Beginning that all other things have, otherwise there would be something peculiar or anomalous or sectarian in its origin, which would destroy its claims to genuineness and catholicity. What, then, is the Beginning of all things and consequently the Beginning of Philosophy?

'Answer—Want.

'Want is the Beginning of Philosophy because it is the Beginning of all things. Is the Beginning of Philosophy a bodily want? No. Why not? Because nothing that may be given to the Body has any effect in appeasing the want. The Beginning of Philosophy, then, must be an intellectual want—a Hunger of the Soul.

'But all wants have their objects in which they seek and find their gratification. What then is the object of the hunger of the soul?

'Answer—Knowledge.

'Philosophy is a Hunger of the Soul after Knowledge. What is Knowledge?—reduced through various intermediate stages to question, what is the common and essential quality in all knowledge—the quality which makes knowledge knowledge? Answer approached by raising question: What is the essential quality in all food—the quality which makes food food? This is obviously its physically nutritive quality. Whatever has the nutritive property is food;

whatever has it not is not food, however like excellent beef and mutton it may be. So in regard to knowledge, its common and essential quality—the quality in virtue of which knowledge is knowledge—is its nutritive quality. Whatever nourishes and satisfies the mind is knowledge, as whatever nourishes and satisfies the body is food. The intellectually *nutritive property* in knowledge is the common and essential property in knowledge. What is the nutritive quality in knowledge? Answer (without beating about the bush)—Truth.

'What is Truth? Answer—Truth is whatever is supported by Evidence.

'What is Evidence? Evidence is whatever is supported by Experience. What is Experience? Here we stop; we can only divide Experience into its kinds, which are two, *Experience of Fact* and *Experience of Pure Reason.* Observe the manœuvre in the last line by which you knaves of the anti-metaphysical school are outwitted. You *oppose Pure Reason* to *Experience,* and philosophers generally assent to the distinction. This at once gives your school the advantage, for the world will always cleave to experience in preference to anything else, leaving us metaphysicians, who are supposed to abandon experience, hanging as it were in baskets in the clouds. But *I* do not abandon experience as the ultimate foundation of *all* knowledge; only I maintain that there are *two* kinds of experience, both of which are equally experience, the experience of Fact and the experience of Pure Reason. You are thus deprived of your advantage. I am as much a man of experience as you are.'

Evidently it had been a question with Ferrier whether he should use the expression Experience, so well known to us now, or substitute for it Consciousness, which, as a matter of fact, he afterwards did: 'Why is it so grievous and fatal an error to confound Experience and Consciousness? Is not a man's experience the whole developed contents of his consciousness? I cannot see how this can be denied. And therefore, before you wrote, I was *swithering* (and am so still) whether I should not make consciousness the basis of the whole superstructure—the raw material of the article which in its finished state is knowledge. After all, the dispute, I suspect, is mainly verbal.'

There are many evidences in these letters that Ferrier was not neglecting German Philosophy, for taking Experience as his basis he shows how it may be divided into *Wesen* (*an sich*), *Seyn* (*für sich*), and the *Begriff* (*anundfürsich*) on the lines of German metaphysics. As to the 'Common-Sense' Philosophy, he expresses himself in no measured terms: 'I am glad we agree in opinion as to the merits of the Common-Sense Philosophy. Considered in its details and accessories, it certainly contains many good things; but, viewed as a whole and *in essentialibus*, it is about the greatest humbug that ever was palmed off upon an unwary world. As an instance among many which might be adduced, of the ambiguity of the word, and of the vacillation of the members of this school, it may be remarked that while Reid made the essence of common-sense to consist in this, that its judgments are not conclusions obtained by ratiocination (*Works*, Sir W. Hamilton's edition, p. 425), Stewart, on the contrary, holds that these judgments are "the result of a train of reasoning so rapid as to escape notice" (*Elements*, vol. ii. p. 103). Sir W.'s *one hundred and six witnesses* are a most conglomerate set, and a little cross-examination would try their mettle severely.'

The most important part of Ferrier's system was his working out of the 'Theory of Ignorance,' in which, indeed, he might congratulate himself in having in great measure broken open new ground. He says of it: 'Hurrah, εὕρηκα, I have discovered the *Law of Ignorance*—and if I had a hecatomb of kain hens at my command I would sacrifice them *instanter* to the propitious patron of metaphysics. Look you here. The Law of Knowledge is this, that, in order to know any *one* thing we must always know two things; *hoc cum alio*—object plus subject—thing + me. This is the unit of knowledge. Analogously, only inversely, in order to be ignorant of any *one* thing we must be ignorant of *two* things—*hujus cum alio*—object plus subject—thing + me. This is the unit of ignorance.' Apparently, in spite of full explanation of his newly-discovered view, Ferrier's correspondent had failed to take it in, and consequently he gently rails at him for 'sticking at the axiom,' and wishes him to help him to a name for what he calls the 'Agnoiology' for want of something better. He goes on: 'I take it that I have caught you in my net, and that wallop about as you will I shall land you at last. I have now little fear that I shall succeed in convincing you, or at anyrate less hardened sinners, that the knowledge of object-subject is a self-contradiction, and that therefore object-subject, or matter *per se*, is not a thing of which we can with any sense or propriety be said to be ignorant. Be this as it may, you must at anyrate recognise in this doctrine a very great novelty in philosophy. The more incogitable a thing becomes, the more ignorant of it do *we* become—that is the natural supposition. Is it not then a bold and original stroke to show that when a thing passes into absolute incogitability we cease that instant to be ignorant of it? I believe that doctrine to be right and true, but I am certain that, obvious as it is, it has been nowhere anticipated or even hinted at in the bygone career of speculation. I claim this as *my discovery*. In the doctrine of Ignorance I believe that I have absolutely no precursor. What think you?'

Mr. Makgill had accused Ferrier of anthropomorphism in his system, and he replies as follows:—'You cannot charge me with anthropomorphism without being guilty of it yourself. Don't you see that "the Beyond" all human thought and knowledge is itself *a category* of human thought? There is much *naïveté* in the procedure of you cautious gentry who would keep scrupulously *within* the length of your tether: as if the conception of a *without* that tether was not a mode of thinking. Will you tell me why you and Kant and others don't make *existence* a category of human thought? This has always puzzled me.

'Surely the man who made extension and time mere forms of human knowledge need have made no bones of existence. Meanwhile, as the post is just starting, I beg you to consider this, that the anthropomorphist and the anti-anthropomorphists are both of necessity anthropomorphists, and for my part I maintain that the anti-man is the bigger anthropomorphist of the two.' This criticism of the 'Beyond' and its unknowableness, while yet it was acknowledged, is as much to the point in the present day as it was in those, and its statement brings forcibly before our minds the truth of Goethe's well-known saying: '*Der Mensch begreift niemals wie anthropomorphisch er ist.*'

The doctrine of Ignorance, so essential to Ferrier's system, he found it hard to make clear to others:—'I am astonished at your not seeing the use, indeed the absolute necessity, of a *true* doctrine of ignorance. This blindness of yours shows me what I may expect from the public; and how careful I must be, if I would go down at all, to render myself perfectly clear and explicit. Don't you see that a correct doctrine of ignorance is necessary for two reasons—*first*, on account of the *false* doctrine of ignorance universally prevalent, one which has hitherto rendered, and must ever render, anything like a scientific ontology impossible; and, *secondly*, because this correct theory of ignorance follows inevitably from my doctrine of knowledge? This, which I consider a very strong recommendation, an indispensable condition of the theory of ignorance, is the very ground on which you object to it. Surely you would not have me establish a doctrine of ignorance which was not consistent with my doctrine of knowledge. Surely I am entitled to deduce all that is logically deducible from my principles. Your meaning I presume is that my doctrine of ignorance flows so manifestly from my doctrine of knowledge that it is unnecessary to develop and parade it. There I differ from you. It flows *inevitably*, but I cannot think that it flows obviously. Else why was it never hit upon until now?... Don't tell me, then, that *my* conclusions that matter *per se*, *Ding an sich*, is what it is impossible for us to be ignorant of, just *because* it is absolutely unknowable (and for no other reason). Don't tell me that this conclusion is so obvious as not to require to be put down in black and white, when we find Kant and *every* other philosopher drawing, but most erroneously, the directly opposite conclusion from the same premises. Matter *per se*, *Ding an sich*, was of all things that of which we were most ignorant!! and the ruin of metaphysics was the consequence of their infatuated blindness. Your objection, then, to my doctrine of ignorance, viz., that it is fixed in the very fixing of the doctrine of knowledge, and therefore does not require explication or elucidation, I cannot regard as a good objection. It is true that the one of these fixes the other; but it requires some amount of explanation and demonstration to make this palpable to the understandings even of the most acute, and I am not sure that even you (yes, put on your best pair of spectacles, you will need them) yet see how impossible it is for us to be ignorant of matter *per se*, or of anything which is absolutely unknowable.'

This matter of the *Ding an sich* Ferrier felt to be the crucial point in his system: 'You talk glibly of "existence *per se*," as maids of fifteen do of puppy dogs. This shows that, like a carpet knight, you have never smelt the real smoke of metaphysical battle, but at most have taken part in the sham fights and listened to the shotless popguns of the martinet of Königsberg. You will find existence *per se* a tougher customer than you imagine.'

As to the *Institutes*, then on the verge of publication, the author says: 'I am inclined to follow your advice, so far, in regard to the title of the work, and to call it the "Theory of Knowing and Being," leaving out ignorance. But why an *introduction* to metaphysics? If this be an *introduction* to metaphysics, pray, Mr. Pundit, what and where are metaphysics themselves? No, sir, it shall be called a *text-book* of metaphysics, meaning thereby, that it is a complete body (and soul) of metaphysics. You are an uncommonly *modest* fellow in so far as the protestations of your *friends* are concerned!'

This correspondence appears to have continued regularly for some years, and to have dealt almost entirely with metaphysical and economic subjects—the subjects which were constantly in Ferrier's mind, as he taught them in the University and tried to work them out in his study. Doubtless it was of the greatest use to him to be able to write about them as he would, had opportunity served, have spoken; and this opportunity was afforded by his friendship with his correspondent, whose interest in philosophy was keen, and whose critical faculties were exceptionally acute, although he never accomplished any original work on philosophical lines.

Of other letters few have been preserved. Absence from home did not make a reason for writing, for Ferrier's journeyings were but few. In 1859, however, he made an expedition to England to see his newly-married daughter, Lady Grant, start for India with her husband, Sir Alexander Grant, after his appointment to the Chancellorship of the University of Bombay. From Southampton he made his way to the scene of his schooldays at Greenwich, from which place he writes to one of the sons of Dr. Bruce of Ruthwell, with whom he spent a happy childhood: 'One of our fêtes was a sumptuous fish dinner at Greenwich. I call it sumptuous, but in truth the fish was utter trash, the best of them not comparable to Loch Fyne herring. Whitebait is the greatest humbug of the age, though it may be heresy to say so in your neighbourhood.' This journey was concluded by a visit to Oxford and to the Lake country, with both of which Ferrier's associations were so many and so agreeable.

The following is a letter, dated 21st March 1862, to Professor Lushington, his friend and biographer:—'I have been very remiss in not acknowledging your photograph, which came safe, and is much admired by all who have seen it. I must get a book for its reception and that of some other worthies, otherwise my children will appropriate it for their collections, with which the house is swarming…. The *ego* is an infinite and active capacity of *never being anything in particular*. I will uphold that definition against the world. Did you never feel how much you revolted from being fixed and determined? Depend upon it, that is the true nature of a spirit—never to be any determinate existence. This is our real immutability—for death can get hold only of that which has a determinate being. *We* stand loose from all determinations. That is our chance of escaping his clutches."

This expresses Ferrier's views and hopes for an after life: he looked forward to an immortality in which the particular and determinate should disappear and only the absolute element remain—in which death should mean only the rising from the individual into a true and universal life. It is a matter to which he frequently refers, and always in terms of a very similar nature. We shall see how, when the end was coming near, his views remained the same, and he was able to face the inevitable without a qualm or shadow of complaint.

CHAPTER VI

FERRIER'S SYSTEM OF PHILOSOPHY—PHILOSOPHICAL WRITINGS

'If one were asked,' says Professor Fraser, 'for the English writings which are fitted in the most attractive way to absorb a reader of competent intelligence and imagination in the final or metaphysical question concerning the Being in which we and the world of sensible things participate, Berkeley's *Dialogues*, Hume's *Inquiry into Human Understanding*, and some of the lately published *Philosophical Remains* of Professor Ferrier are probably those which would best deserve to be mentioned.'

It has been given to few philosophers of modern days to write on philosophic questions in a manner at once so lucid and so convincing as that of Ferrier. Nor can it in his case be said that matter is sacrificed to form, for the writer does not hesitate to 'nail his colours to the mast,' as he himself expresses it, and to tackle questions the most vital in their character in a straightforward and uncompromising fashion. His earliest published writings, as we have seen, took the form of a series of seven articles, which appeared, roughly speaking, in alternate months, between February of 1838 and March of 1839. These articles, entitled *An Introduction to the Philosophy of Consciousness*, represented the results of their author's work during the years which had elapsed since he first began to be really interested in philosophy, and to feel that the way of looking at it adopted almost universally in Scotland was not satisfying to himself, or in any way defensible.

The whole point in Ferrier's view turns upon the way in which we look at 'Mind.' 'The human mind, to speak it profanely,' says Ferrier, 'is like the goose that laid the golden eggs. The metaphysician resembles the analytic poulterer who slew it to get at them in a lump, and found *nothing* for his pains.... Look at thought, and feeling, and passion, as they glow in the pages of Shakespeare— golden eggs indeed! Look at the same as they stagnate on the dissecting-table of Dr. Brown, and marvel at the change. Behold how shapeless and extinct they have become!' Locke began by saying there are no original ideas, simply impressions from without; Hume then says cause and effect are incapable of explanation, and the notion which we form of them is a nonentity, seeing that we have a series of impressions alone to work from; Reid says there is a mind and there is an object, and calls in common-sense to interpret between the two. But the mistake all through is very evident: man looks at Nature in a certain way, interprets her by certain categories, and then he turns his eye upon himself, endeavouring thereby to judge of what he finds within by methods of a similar kind. And the human mind cannot be so 'objectised'; it is something more than the sum of its 'feelings,' 'passions,' and 'states of mind.' Dr. Reid had done a service by exploding the old doctrine of 'ideas'; he brought mind into contact with immediate things, but much more is left for us to do; the same office has to be performed for 'mind'—that is, mind when we regard it as something which connects us with the universe, or something which can be looked at and examined, as we might look at or examine a thing outside ourselves, and not as that which is necessary to any such examination. 'Is it not enough for a man that he is *himself*? There can be no dispute about that. *I* am; what more would I have? What more would I be? Why would I be *mind*? I am *myself* therefore let it perish.'

What, then, makes a man what he is? It is the fact of consciousness, the fact which marks him off from all other things with a deep line of separation. It is this and this alone, Ferrier says, this '*human* phenomenon,' and not its objects, passions, or emotions, which leads us into pastures fresh and far separated from the dreary round which the old metaphysicians followed. The same discovery, of course, is always being made, though to Ferrier it was new; we are always straying into devious ways, ways that lead us into grey regions of abstraction, and we always want to be called back to the concrete and the real, to the freshness and the brightness of life as it is and lives.

Ferrier from this time onwards, from his youth until his death, kept one definite aim in view: the object of his life was to insist with all his might that our interests must be concentrated on man as he is as man, and not on a mere sum-total of passions and sensations by which the human being is affected. The consciousness of a state of mind is very different from that state of mind itself, and the two must be kept absolutely distinct. 'Let mind have the things which are mind's, and man the things which are man's.' We should, Ferrier says, fling 'mind' and its lumber overboard, busy ourselves with *the man* and his facts. Man's passions and sensations may be referred to 'mind' indeed, but he cannot lay his hands upon the fact of consciousness. That fact cannot be conceived of as vested in the *object* called the 'human mind,' an object being something really or ideally different from ourselves. In speaking of 'my mind,' mind may be what it chooses, but the consciousness is in the *ego*; and mind is really destitute of consciousness, otherwise the *ego* would necessarily be present in it. The dilemma is as follows: 'Unless the philosophers of mind attribute consciousness to mind, they leave out of view the most important phenomena of man; and *if* they attribute consciousness to mind, they annihilate the object of their research, in so far as the whole extent of this fact is concerned.'

Since Ferrier's time this point has been worked out very fully, and by none more successfully than by an English philosopher, Professor T. H. Green of Oxford, in his Introduction to the works of Hume. But when Ferrier wrote, his ideas were new; in England at least he was breaking up ground hitherto untouched, and therefore the debt of gratitude we owe him is not small, especially when we consider the forces against which he warred. 'Common-sense,' the solution offered for all philosophic difficulties, is really the *problem* of philosophy, and to speak of the 'philosophy of common-sense' is simply to confuse the problem with its solution. Common-sense, or rather what is given by its means, has simply to be construed into intelligible forms: in itself it makes no attempt to solve the difficulties that present themselves, and it is folly to suggest its doing so. When a man speaks of *my* sensations or *my* states of mind, he means something of which he—as consciousness—is independent, and which can be made an object to him. Were it not so, of course he could not possibly arrive at freedom, but would merely be the helpless child of destiny; and, as Ferrier points out, were consciousness and sensation one, consciousness would not have the power, undoubtedly possessed by it, of 'recovering the balance' that it loses on experiencing pain or passion; the return of consciousness, as he puts it, 'lowers the temperature' of the sensation or the passion, and the man regains the personality that for the time had almost vanished. A man, he tells us, can hardly even be said to be the 'victim' of his mind, and irresponsible—*i.e.*, man stands aloof from the modifications which may visit him, therefore we should study him as he is, and not merely these 'states of mind' common to him and to animals alike. And consciousness must be active, exercising itself upon those states, and thereby realising human freedom.

Philosophy, then, is the gospel of freedom as contrasted with the bondage of the physical kingdom. But we are in subjection at the first, and all our lifetime a constant fight is being carried on. Philosophy paints its grey in grey, another great philosopher has told us, only when the freshness and life of youth has gone: the reconciliation is in the ideal, not the actual world. And so with Ferrier: 'The flowers of thy happiness,' says he, 'are withered. They could not last; they gilded but for a day the opening portals of life. But in their place I will give thee freedom's flowers. To act *according* to thy inclination may be enjoyment; but know that to act *against* it is liberty, and thou only actest thus because thou art really free.' Great and weighty words, which might be pondered by many more than those to whom they were originally addressed.

Having established his fundamental principles, Ferrier goes on to trace the birth of self-consciousness in the child—the knowledge of itself as 'I,' which means the knowledge of good and evil—the moral birth. Perception, again, is a synthesis of sensation and consciousness—the realisation of self in conjunction with the sensation experienced: it is, of course, peculiar to man. Things can only take effect on 'me' when there is a 'me' to take effect upon, and not at birth, or before I come to consciousness. Consciousness is the very essence and origin of the *ego*; without consciousness no man would be 'I.' It is our refusal to be acted on by outside impressions that constitutes our personality and perception of them; our communication with the universe is the communication of *non-*communication. And the *ego* is not something which comes into the world ready-made; it is a living activity which is *never* passive, for were it passive, it would be annihilated; in submitting to the action of causality its life would be gone. Our destiny is to free ourselves from the bonds of nature, from that 'blessed state of primeval innocence,' the blessedness, after all, of bondage. A man cannot *be* until he *acts*, for his Being arises out of his actions: consciousness being an act, our proper existence is the consequence of that act. His natural condition for others, and before he comes to existence, Ferrier says, is given, while his existence for himself is made by his thinking himself. It is only in the latter case that he can attain to Liberty, instead of remaining bound by the bonds imposed upon him by Necessity. The three great moments of humanity are: first, the natural or given man in enslaved Being; second, the conscious man in action working into freedom against passion; third, the 'I': man as free, that is, real personal Being.

Philosophy has thus a great future before her. Instead of being a mere dead theory as heretofore, she becomes renovated into a new life when she gets her proper place; she is separated from her supposed connection with the physical world, and is recognised as consciousness. When this is so, she loses her merely theoretic aspect, and is identified with the living practical interests of mankind. The dead symbols become living realities, the dead twigs are clothed with verdure. 'Know thyself, and in knowing thyself thou shalt see that this self is not thy true self; but, in the very act of knowing this, thou shalt at once displace this false self, and establish thy true self in its room.' And Ferrier goes on to trace the bearings of his theories in the moral and intellectual world. He finds in morality something more than a refined self-love; he finds the dawning will endeavouring to assert itself, to break free from the trammels imposed upon it by nature. Freedom, the great end of man, is contravened by the passive conditions of his nature; these are therefore wrong, and every act of resistance tends to the accomplishment of the one important end, which is to procure his liberty.

This essay, or series of essays, gives the keynote to Ferrier's thought and writings, therefore it seemed worth while to consider its argument in detail. The completeness of the break with the old philosophy is manifest. The 'scientific' methods applied to every region of knowledge were then in universal use, and no little courage was required to challenge their pretensions as they were challenged by Ferrier. But in courage, as we know, Ferrier was never lacking. His mind once made up, he had no fear in making his opinions known. He considered that the Scottish Philosophy had become something very like materialism in the hands of Brown and others, and he believed that the whole point of view must be changed if a really spiritual philosophy was to take its place. There may be traces of the impetuosity of youth in this attack: much working out was undoubtedly required before it could be said that a system had been established. But all the same this essay is a brilliant piece of philosophic writing—instinct with life and enthusiasm—one which must have made its readers feel that the dry bones of a dead system had wakened into life, and that what they had imagined an abstract and dismal science had become instinct with living, practical interest—something to be 'lived' as well as studied.

The *Institutes of Metaphysics*—the work by which Ferrier's name will descend to posterity—is a development of the Philosophy of Consciousness; but it is more carefully reasoned out and systematised—the result of many years of thoughtful labour. For several years before the work was published (in 1854) the propositions which are contained in it were developed in the course of Ferrier's regular lectures. The *Institutes*, or *Theory of Knowing and Being*, commences with a definition of philosophy as a 'body of reasoned truth,' and states that though there were plenty of dissertations on the subject in existence, there was no philosophy itself—no scheme of demonstrated truth; and this, and not simply a 'contribution' to philosophy was what was now required, and what the writer proposed to give. The divisions into which he separates Philosophy are: first, the Epistemology, or theory of knowledge; secondly, the Agnoiology, or theory of ignorance; and thirdly, the Ontology, or theory of being. The fundamental question is, 'What is the *one* feature which is identical, invariable, and essential in all the varieties of our knowledge?'

The first condition of knowledge is that we should know ourselves, and reason gives certainty to this proposition which is not capable of demonstration, owing to its being itself the starting-point; the counter-proposition, asserting the separate subject and object of knowledge, and the mutual presence of the two without intelligence's being necessarily cognisant of itself, represents general opinion, and the ordinary view of popular psychology. Knowledge, then, Ferrier goes on, always has the self as an essential part of it; it is knowledge-in-union-with-whatever-it-apprehends. The objective part of the object of knowledge, though distinguishable, is not really separable from the subjective or *ego*; both constitute the *unit* of knowledge—an utterance thoroughly Hegelian in its character, however Ferrier may disclaim a connection with Hegel's system. In space they may be separated, but not in cognition, and this idealism does not for one moment deny the existence of 'external' things, but only says they can have no meaning if out of relation to those which are 'internal'; as Hegel might have put it, they could be known as separable by means of 'abstraction' only. From this point we are led on to the next statement, and a most important statement it is, that matter *per se* is of necessity absolutely unknowable; or to what Ferrier calls the Theory of Ignorance. Whether or not this theory can make good the title to originality which its author claims for it, there is no doubt that its statement in clear language, such as no one can fail to understand, marks an important era in English speculation. There are, Ferrier says, two sorts of so-called ignorance: one of these is incidental to some minds, but not to all—an ignorance of defect, he puts it—just as we might be said to be ignorant of a language we had never learned. But the other ignorance (not, properly speaking, ignorance at all) is incident to *all* intelligence by its very nature, and is no defect or imperfection. The law of ignorance hence is that 'we can be ignorant only of what can be known,' or 'the knowable is alone the ignorable.' The bearing of this important point is seen at once when we turn back to the theory of knowing. Knowledge is something of which the subject cannot shake himself free; 'I' must always, in whatever I apprehend, apprehend 'me.' We don't apprehend 'things,' that is, but what is apprehended is 'me-apprehending-things.' Things-plus-me is the only knowable, and consequently the only 'ignorable.'

This brings us a great way towards the Absolute Idealism associated mainly with the name of Hegel—towards the Knowledge or 'Experience' (a word which Ferrier afterwards himself makes use of) which shall cease to be a 'theory,' being recognised as comprehending within itself all Reality—as recognising no distinction between object and subject, excepting when they are regarded as two poles both equally essential, and separated only when looked at in abstraction. If Ferrier's 'theory of knowledge' did not proceed so far, he at least made the discovery that the subjective idealism of Kant was as unsatisfactory as the relativity of Hamilton, and as certainly tending to agnosticism. Kant's 'thing-in-itself' is not that of which we are ignorant, or a hidden reality which can be known by faith. It is that which cannot possibly be known—and, in other words, a contradiction or nonsense. Now, Ferrier says, we arrive at the true Idealism—the triumph of philosophy. If it is said to reduce all things to the phenomena of consciousness, it does the same to every *nothing*. What falls out of consciousness becomes incogitable; it lapses, not into nothing, but into what is contradictory. The material universe *per se*, and all its qualities *per se*, are not only absolutely unknowable, but absolutely unthinkable. We do indeed know substance, but only as object plus subject—as matter *mecum* or in cognition as thought together with the self.

It may be true that we cannot claim for Ferrier complete originality in his thinking; work on very similar lines was being carried on elsewhere. It is not difficult to trace throughout his writings the mode of his development. The earlier works are evidently influenced by Fichte and his school, since the personal *ego* and individual freedom figure as the principal conceptions in our knowledge; and even while the Scottish school of psychologists is being combated, the influence of Hamilton is very manifest. But as time goes on, Ferrier's ideas become more concrete; the theory of consciousness becomes more absolute in its conception; the human or individual element is less conspicuous as the universal element is more, which signifies that gradually he approaches closer to the standpoint of the later German thinkers by a careful study of their works, though for the most part it is Reid and Hamilton his criticisms have in view, and not the corresponding work of Kant.

Still, we should say that Ferrier's attitude represented another phase in the same struggle against abstraction and towards unity in knowledge, rather than being a simple outcome of the German influence in Scotland. This last assumption he at least repudiated with energy, and boldly claimed to have developed and completed his system for himself. He claimed to have worked on national lines; to have started from the philosophy of his country as it was currently accepted, and to have little difficulty in proving from itself its absolute inadequacy. He felt that in his doctrine of the reality of knowledge he had found the means of solving problems hitherto dark and obscure, and he used his instruments bravely, and on the whole successfully.

The faith-philosophy which professed to know reality through the senses, when these senses were a part of the external universe, or signified taking for granted the matter in dispute, was utterly repugnant to Ferrier. The Unknowable of Sir William Hamilton was inconceivable to him, and he ever kept this theory and its errors in his mind, while developing a system of his own. It is better that a philosophic system should grow up thus, instead of coming to us from without in language hard to understand because of foreign idioms and unwonted modes of expression. To be of use, a philosophy should speak the language of the people: until it becomes identified with ordinary ways of thinking, its influence is never really great; and the Idealism of Germany has in this country always suffered from being intelligible only to the few. Therefore we hold all credit due to Ferrier for consistently refusing to adopt the phraseology of a foreign country, and setting himself, heart and soul, to find expression for his thoughts in the language of his birth.

Ferrier introduces his *Lectures on Greek Philosophy*, the last subject on which he undertook to write, in a manner which reminds us of Hegel's remarkable Introduction to his *History of Philosophy*; he begins, like Hegel, by pointing out that the study of philosophy is just the study of our own reason in its development, but that what is worked out in our minds hurriedly and within contracted limits, is in philosophy evolved at leisure, and seen in its just proportions: the historian of philosophy has not merely to record the existence of dead systems of thought that are past and gone, but the living products of his *own*, full of present, vital interest, and there is nothing arbitrary or capricious in such a history: all is reasoned thought as it manifests and reveals itself.

Philosophy, Ferrier defines, by calling it the pursuit of Truth—not relative Truth, but absolute, what necessarily exists for all minds alike; and man's faculties (contrary to what is generally supposed) are competent to attain to it, provided only that they have something in common with all other minds, *i.e.*, are partakers in a universal intelligence. He works this out in his Introduction in an extremely interesting way, showing, as he does, how in all intelligence there must be a universal, a unity; that the very essence of religion, for example, rests on the unity which constitutes the bond between God and man, and that when this is denied, religion is made impossible. What then, we may ask, is the Truth that has to be pursued?

It is that which is the real, the object of philosophy—the real which exists for all intelligence. The historian of philosophy must show that philosophy in its history corresponds with this definition, if the definition be a true one.

The lectures begin with Thales and the followers of the Ionic school, and Ferrier points out how, in spite of the material elements which are taken as a basis, their systems are philosophic, in so far as they aim at the establishment of a universal in all things, and carry with them the belief that this universal is the ultimately real; and this gives them an interest which from their sensuous forms we could hardly have expected to find. But it was Heraclitus' doctrine of Becoming that was most congenial to Ferrier, as it was to his great predecessor Hegel. Being and Not-Being, the unity of contraries as essential sides of Truth, in such conceptions as these Ferrier believes we come nearer to the truth of the universe than in the current views of philosophy, in which the unity of contrary determinations in one subject is regarded as impossible. Apart, either side is incomprehensible, and hence Mr. Mansel and Sir William Hamilton argue the impotence of human reason; but if, as Ferrier believes, they are shown to be but moments or essential factors in conception, the antagonism will be proved unreal—it will be an antagonism proper to the very life and essence of reason.

Possibly in his account of the early Greek philosophers Ferrier may have done what many historians of philosophy have done before him, he may have read into the systems which he has been describing much more than he was entitled so to read. He may, when he is talking of the Eleatics of Heraclitus, and even of Socrates and Plato, have had before his mind the special battle which he had chosen to fight—the battle against sensationalism in Scotland, against materialism in the form in which he found it—rather than fairly to set before his readers an exact and accurate account of the teaching of the particular philosopher of whom he writes. But has it ever been otherwise in any history of thought that was ever written, excepting perhaps in some dryasdust compendium which none excepting those weighed down with dread of examination questions, care to peruse? Thought reads itself from itself, and if it sometimes reads the present into the past, and thinks to see it there, is there matter for surprise, or is it so very far wrong? If it tells us something of the secrets it itself conceals, it is surely telling us after all much of those that are gone.

For Plato, Ferrier naturally had a very great affinity; he deals with him at length, and evidently had made a special and careful study of his writings. But the same method is applied by him to Plato as was before applied to the other Greek philosophers. 'It is not so much by reading Plato as by studying our own minds that we can find out what ideas are, and perceive the significance of the theory which expounds them. It is only by verifying in our own consciousness the discoveries of antecedent philosophers that we can hope rightly to understand their doctrines or appreciate the value and importance of their speculations.' And so Ferrier proceeds to prove the necessity for the existence of 'ideas'—of universals—as the absolute truth and groundwork of whatever is. No intelligence can be intelligent excepting by their light, and they are the necessary laws or principles on which all Being and Knowing are dependent. 'All philosophy,' he says of Plato, 'speculative and practical, has been foreshadowed by his prophetic intelligence; often dimly, but always so attractively as to whet the curiosity and stimulate the ardour of those who have chosen him as a guide.' And it was as such that Ferrier marked him out and chose him as his own. With Aristotle he had probably less in common, and his treatment both of him and of the Stoics, Epicureans, and Neo-Platonists, with which the history ends, is less sympathetic in its tone and understanding in its style. But these lectures as a whole, though never put together for printing as a book, must always be of interest to the student of philosophy.

A philosophic article, entitled *Berkeley and Idealism*, and published in June of 1842, was designed to meet the attack of Mr. Samuel Bailey, who had written a *Review of Berkeley's Theory of Vision*, criticising the soundness of his views. Mr. Bailey replied, and Ferrier a year later published an article on that reply. Ferrier rightly appreciates the very important place which ought to be allowed to Berkeley as a factor in the development of philosophic truth—a place which has only been properly understood in later years. He saw the part he had played in bringing the real significance of Absolute Idealism into view, and deprecated the representation of his system made by David Hume, or the popular idea that Berkeley denied all reality to matter. What he did deny was the reality which is supposed to lie beyond experience, and his criticism in this regard was invaluable as a basis for a future system. In his own words, he did not wish to change things into ideas, but *ideas* into *things*: matter could not exist independently of mind. But yet Ferrier is perfectly aware that Berkeley did not entirely grasp the absolute standpoint that the thing is the appearance, and the appearance is the thing. Regarded merely as a literary production, this article is entitled to rank with the classics of philosophic writings both as regards the beauty of its style and its logical development. Ferrier does not often touch directly on questions of religion or theology, but there is an interesting passage in this essay which shows his views regarding the question of immortality. He is talking of the impossibility of our ever conceiving to ourselves the idea of our annihilation. Such an idea could not be rationally articulated. We *appear*, indeed, to be able to realise it, but we only *think* we think it: real thought of death in this sense would involve our being already dead; but in thought we are and must be immortal. 'We have nothing to wait for; eternity is even now within us, and time, with all its vexing troubles, is no more.'

It was something absolute and enduring for which Ferrier was ever on the search. Those of his Introductory Lectures which are preserved bear out this statement, if nothing else were left to do so. Philosophy, thought, is more than systems: 'As long as man thinks, the light must burn.' Could he but teach the young men who gathered round him day by day to think, he cared little as to what so-called 'system' they adopted. He put his arguments clearly before them, but they were free to criticise as they would. And perhaps it was because they realised that the Truth was more to him than personal fame that their affection for him was so great. He always kept before him, too, that in teaching any science the mental discipline which it involves must not be overlooked. The practical rule of disciplining the mind should run side by side with the theoretical instruction, which might soon be forgotten; the great effort of a teacher should be in the best and highest sense to *educate* his students. That is, he has not only to instil their minds with multifarious learning, but to make their thinking systematic.

And philosophy must, he tells us, be made interesting if it is to be of any use: we must arrive at a 'philosophic consciousness,' and distinguish philosophy from mere opinion. It is mind which is the permanent and immutable in all change and mutation; even the Greeks found the idea of permanence in mind while they regarded change as the principle of matter.

Thus, when the end of the day had come, when the lamp grew dim, and the books he loved so much must be for the last time shut, Ferrier's teaching was not so very different from what it was nearly thirty years before. The only real change was that the impetuosity of youth had gone; the man and his system had both become matured: the one more tolerant, more careful in expression, more considerate of the feelings of his opponents; the other more systematic, more coordinated, firmer in its grasp. There was much to do if the system were to be shown to hold its place in every department of life, as an absolute system must: much that has not even yet been accomplished. But for those who came in contact with him, the man was more even than his creed—to them this frail form which seemed to be wasting away before their eyes, yet never losing the keen interest in work to be accomplished, must have taught a lesson more than systems of philosophy dream of. For they could not fail to learn that the eternal can be found in history—even in history of long centuries ago, as in every other sphere of knowledge—and that the search for it supports the seeker in his daily life, takes all its bitterness from what is hardest, from pain, suffering, and even death.

CHAPTER VII

THE COLERIDGE PLAGIARISM—MISCELLANEOUS LITERARY WORK

The story of the so-called Coleridge plagiarism is an old one now, but it is one which roused much feeling at the time, and likewise one on which there is considerable division of opinion even in the present day. Into this controversy Ferrier plunged by writing a formidable indictment of Coleridge's position in *Blackwood's Magazine* for March of 1840.

When Ferrier took up the cudgels the matter stood thus. In the earlier quarter of the century German Philosophy was coming, or rather had already come, more or less into vogue in England; and as the German language was not largely read, and yet people were vaguely interested, though in what they hardly knew, they welcomed an appreciative interpreter of that philosophy, and an original writer on similar lines, in one whose reputation was esteemed so highly as that of Coleridge. Coleridge in this matter, indeed, occupied a position which was unique; for the treasures of German poetry and prose had not as yet been fully opened up, and he was held to possess the means of doing this in a quite exceptional degree. The works of Schiller, Goethe, and the other poets came to the world—and to Coleridge with the rest—as a sort of revelation. But the poet in his own mind was nothing if not a philosopher—a kind of seer amongst men, speculating, somewhat vaguely it might be, on matters of transcendental import—and in Schelling he thought he had discovered a kindred spirit; in his writings he believed he had found the Idealism for which he had so long been seeking in Böhme, Fox, and the other mystics—a creed which, though pantheistic in its essence, yet fulfilled the condition of being both orthodox and Trinitarian in its form. This, for many reasons, was a creed presenting many attractions to the younger men of the day, especially when set forth with a certain literary flavour. We have Carlyle's immortal picture of how it influenced John Sterling and his friends.

Coleridge's *Biographia Literaria*, in which the principal so-called Schelling plagiarisms are contained, was published in 1817, but it was not for a considerable time after that that the plagiarisms were discovered, or at least taken notice of. The first serious indictment came from no less an authority than De Quincey, whose interest in philosophical matters was as great as Coleridge's, and who published his views in an appreciative but gossipy article in *Tait's Magazine* of September 1834. To commence with, he took up the question of the 'Hymn to Chamouni'; but since, in this matter, Coleridge afterwards admitted his indebtedness to a German poetess, Frederica Brun, it does not seem an important one. Nor, indeed, does De Quincey pretend to take exception to certain expressions in Coleridge's 'France' which are evidently borrowed from Milton, or to regard them as indicating more than a peculiar omission of quotation marks. But the really serious matter, one for which De Quincey cannot by any means account, is that in the *Biographia Literaria* there occurs a dissertation on the doctrine of Knowing and Being which is an exact translation from an essay written by Schelling. De Quincey cannot indeed explain away the mystery, but he makes the best of it, pleading excuses such as we often hear

51

adduced in cases of 'kleptomania' when they occur amongst the well-to-do, or so-called higher classes—*e.g.*, the evident fact that there was no necessity so to steal, no motive for stealing, even though the theft had evidently been committed. Still, though the defence may be ingenious, and though we may go so far as to acknowledge that Coleridge had sufficient originality of mind to weave out theories of his own without borrowing from others, it must be confessed that under the aggravated circumstances the argument falls somewhat flat; and this was the impression made on many minds even at the time. The ball once set rolling, the dispute went on, and the next important incident was an article by Julius Hare in the *British Magazine* of January 1835. This is a hot defence of the so-called 'Christian' philosopher, who is said to be influencing the best and most promising young men of the day, as against the assault of the 'English Opium-Eater'—'that ill-boding *alias* of evil record.' As to De Quincey's somewhat unkind but entertaining stories, there is some reason in Hare's objections, seeing that they were told of one to whom the writer owned himself indebted. But when Hare tackles the plagiarisms themselves, and endeavours to defend them, his task is harder. Coleridge had indeed stated that his ideas were thought out and matured before he had seen a page of Schelling; but at the same time, in an earlier portion of his work, he made a somewhat ambiguous reference to his indebtedness to the German philosopher, and deprecated his being accused of intentioned plagiarism from his writings. Of course it may be said that a thief does not draw attention to the goods from which he has stolen, but yet even Hare acknowledges that it is hard to understand how half a dozen pages (we now know that it really exceeded thirty) should have been bodily transferred from one work to another, and suggests that the most probable solution is that Coleridge had a practice of keeping notebooks for his thoughts, mingled with extracts from what he had been reading at the time, and that he thus became confused between the two.

At this point Ferrier steps in and takes the whole matter under review—a matter which he looked upon as serious (perhaps more serious than we should now consider it) from a national as well as an individual point of view. He held that the reputation of his country was at stake, as well as that of a single philosophic thinker, and that neither De Quincey nor Hare had gone into the matter with sufficient care or knowledge, or ascertained how large it really was. It was undoubtedly the case that Coleridge's reputation in philosophic matters— and in these days that reputation was not small—was derived from what he had purloined from the writings of a German youth, and whatever the poet's claim on our regard on other scores may be, it was certainly due to Schelling that the debt should be acknowledged. As far as the *Biographia Literaria* is concerned, the facts are plain. Coleridge makes certain general acknowledgments of indebtedness to Schelling to begin with. He acknowledges that there may be found in his works an identity of thought or phrase with Schelling's, and allows him to be the founder of the philosophy of nature; but he claims at the same time the honour of making that philosophy intelligible to his fellow-countrymen, and even of thinking it out beforehand. Having said so much, there follow pages together—sometimes as many as six or eight on end—which are virtually copied *verbatim* from Schelling, though with occasional interpolations of the so-called author here and there. Ferrier has examined the whole matter most minutely, and made a long list of the more flagrant cases of copying: thirty-one pages, he points out, are faithfully transcribed, partially or wholly, from Schelling's works alone, without allowing for what the author admits to be translated *in part* from a 'contemporary writer of the Continent.' And Schelling was not the only sufferer, nor was it only in the region of metaphysics that the thefts were made. The substratum of a whole chapter of the *Biographia Literaria* is, Ferrier discovered, taken from another author named Maasz, and Coleridge's lecture 'On Poesy or Art' is closely copied and largely translated from Schelling's 'Discourse upon the Relations in which the Plastic Arts stand to Nature.' This was a blow indeed to those who had boasted of the profundity of Coleridge's views on art; but his poetry surely remained intact. But no, 'Verses exemplifying the Homeric Metre' are found to be—unacknowledged—a translation from Schiller; and yet worse, because less likely to be discovered, the lines written 'To a Cataract' have the same metre, language, and thought as certain verses by Count von Stolberg, which were shown to Ferrier by a friend.

The whole matter is a very strange one and not easy to explain. Of course the references to Schelling's labours in similar lines are there, and may in a sense disarm our criticism. But then, unfortunately, there also are the statements that the ideas had been matured in Coleridge's mind before he had seen a single line of Schelling's work, and he clearly gives us to understand that he had toiled out the system for himself, and that it was the 'offspring of his own spirit.' It is this overmuch protesting that makes us, like Ferrier, disposed to take the darkest view of the affair: anything that can be said in Coleridge's defence is found in the manner in which it was taken by the one who had most right to feel aggrieved. In the life of Jowett,[10] recently published, there is an interesting account of Schelling's views on Coleridge, taken from a conversation, notes of which were made by the late Sir Alexander Grant, Ferrier's son-in-law, when still an undergraduate. Jowett, while at Berlin, had, it appears, seen Schelling, and talked to him of the plagiarisms. He took the matter, Jowett states, good-naturedly, thought Coleridge to have been attacked unfairly, and even went so far as to assert that he had expressed many things better than he could have done himself—certainly a very generous acknowledgment. Probably the most charitable construction we can put on Coleridge's act is that which Jowett himself advances in saying that the poet is not to be looked upon or judged as an ordinary man would be, seeing that often enough he hardly could be said to have been responsible for his actions; while his egotism, which was extreme, may have likewise led him—it may be almost unconsciously—into acts of doubtful honesty. But evidently, in spite of Ferrier's work, Jowett, and possibly even Schelling himself, had no idea of the extent to which the plagiarisms extended. There would, of course, have been comparatively little harm in Coleridge's action had he been content to borrow materials which he was about to work up in his own way, or to do what his biographer Gillman says is done by the 'bee which flies from flower to flower in quest of food,' but which 'digests and elaborates' that food by its native power. Unfortunately, the more we read

Coleridge's philosophic writings, the more we feel constrained to agree with Ferrier that the matter is not digested as Gillman suggests, but taken possession of in its ready-made condition. The parts which he adds do not assist in throwing light on what precedes, but are evidently padding of a somewhat commonplace and superficial kind. We can only say, like Jowett, that the manner of his life may have injured Coleridge's moral sense, and that his desire to pose as a philosopher who should yet be a so-called 'Christian' may have led him to encroach upon the spheres of others, instead of keeping to those in which he could hold his own unchallenged.

A labour of love with Ferrier, on very different lines than the above, was to bring out in five volumes the works of his father-in-law, John Wilson, 'Christopher North,' including the *Noctes Ambrosianæ*, and his Essays and Papers contributed to *Blackwood*. This was published in 1856, but must, of course, have meant a considerable amount of work to the editor for some time previously. One of the most interesting parts of the work is Ferrier's preface to the famous 'Chaldee Manuscript,' in vol. iv. The story of the 'Chaldee MS.' is now a matter of history, fully recorded in the recently published records of the famous house of Blackwood. In 1817 the Whigs ruled in matters literary, mainly through the instrumentality of the *Edinburgh Review*, then in its heyday of fame. A reaction, however, set in, and the change was inaugurated by the publication of the so-called 'Chaldee MS.,' a wild *extravaganza*, or *jeu d'esprit*, hitting off the foibles of Whiggism, under the guise of an allegory describing the origin and rise of *Blackwood's Magazine*, the rival which had risen up in opposition to the *Review*, and the discomfiture of another journal carried on under the auspices of Constable. It was in the seventh number of *Blackwood* that the satire appeared— that is, the first number of *Blackwood's Edinburgh Magazine* as distinguished from the *Edinburgh Monthly Magazine*, published from Blackwood's office to begin with, but on comparatively mild and inoffensive lines. One may imagine the effect of this Tory outburst on the society of Edinburgh. All the *literati* of the town were involved: Sir Walter Scott himself, Mackenzie, Sir David Brewster, Sir William Hamilton, Professor Jamieson, Tytler, Playfair, and many others, some of whom emerged but seldom from the retirement of private life. Nowadays it would be difficult, if not impossible, to identify the different characters, were it not for the assistance of Professor Ferrier's marginal notes; but in those days they were no doubt recognisable enough. Of course the magazine went like wildfire; but the ludicrous description in semi-biblical language of individuals with absurd allegorical appendages, constituted, as Ferrier acknowledges, an offence against propriety which could not be defended, even though no real malevolence might be signified. Whether Ferrier was justified in republishing the *Noctes*, in so far as they could be identified with Wilson, has been disputed; but, as the publisher, Major Blackwood, points out, the time was past for anyone to be hurt by the personalities which they contained, and the only harm the republication could inflict was upon the *Noctes* themselves. The conception of the 'Chaldee Manuscript,' he tells us, was in the first part due to Hogg; and Wilson and Lockhart were held responsible for the last. There is a tradition, too, though Ferrier does not mention it, that Hamilton was one of the party in Mr. Wilson's house (53 Queen Street) where the skit was said to have been concocted, and that he even contributed to it a verse. This may have been the case, as Wilson and Lockhart were his intimate friends; but it seems strange to think of so thoroughgoing a Whig being found mixed up in such a plot, and with such companions.

Though it is easy to understand that Ferrier felt the editing of his father-in-law and uncle's work was a duty which it was incumbent upon him to perform, one cannot help surmising that it may have been a less congenial task to him than many others. There was little in common between the two men, both distinguished in their way, and Wilson's humour and poetic fancy, however bright and vivid, was not of the sort that would appeal most to Ferrier. A few years before his death Ferrier gave up the project he had in view of writing Wilson's life, partly in despair of setting forth his talents as he felt they should be set forth, and partly from the lack of material to work from. He says, in a letter written at the time, 'It would do no good to talk in general terms of his wonderful powers, of his genius being greater (as in some sense it was) than that of any of his contemporaries—greater, too, than any of his publications show. The public would require other evidences of this beyond one's mere word— something might have been done had some of us Boswellized him judiciously, but this having been omitted, I do not see how it is possible to do him justice.' The book was eventually undertaken, and successfully accomplished, by Wilson's daughter, Mrs. Gordon.

We have spoken of Ferrier's interest in German literature; so early as 1839 he published a translation of *Pietro d'Abano* by Ludwig Tieck, one of the inner circle of the so-called Romantic School to which the Schlegels and Novalis also belonged—the school which opposed itself to the eighteenth-century enlightenment, making its cry the return to nature, and demanding with Fichte that a work of art should be a 'free product of the inner consciousness.' Another specimen of Ferrier's translating powers is given in a rendering from Deinhardstein's *Bild der Danœ*, a love story in which Salvator Rosa figures. This appeared in *Blackwood* of September 1841, and an extract from it is published in the *Remains*.

But one of the earliest and most remarkable of Ferrier's literary criticisms in *Blackwood's Magazine* was an anonymous article on the various translations of Goethe's *Faust* published in 1840. We have seen that Ferrier had made a special study of the writings of Schiller and Goethe, and that his work had been much appreciated both by Lytton and De Quincey. In this article the writer takes seven different renderings of the drama, carefully analyses them, points out their deficiencies, and even adventures on the difficult task, for a critic, of himself translating one or two pages. Now that German is so widely read in England, we are all too well aware of the insufficiency of any translation of *Faust* to regard even the best in any other light than as a makeshift. But then things were different, and it was possible that wrong impressions of the original might be conveyed by inadequate translations. Ferrier's point was that Goethe, while writing in rhyme and in exquisitely poetical language, managed at the same time to find words such as might really be used by ordinary mortals; but the translators, in endeavouring rightly enough to keep to the rhyming form, entirely fail in their endeavour after the same end. He considers that though in prose we may deviate from the ordinary proprieties of language, we may not do so in rhyming poetry; for though the poet has to describe the thought and passion of real men in the language of real life, his dialect must at the same time be taken out of the category of ordinary discourse because of the use of rhyme; and he is therefore called upon as far as possible to remove this bar, and reconcile us to the peculiarity of his style by the simplicity of his language; otherwise all illusion will be at an end. Rhymes brought together by force can succeed in giving us no pleasure; the writer should possess the power of mastering his material and compelling it to serve his ends.

Ferrier's speculative instincts naturally led him to discuss the often-discussed motive of the play. Is it so, as Coleridge says, that the love of knowledge for itself could not bring about the evil consequences depicted in the character of Faust, but only the love of knowledge for some base purpose? Ferrier replies, No, the love of knowledge as an end in itself would people the world with Fausts. 'Such a love of knowledge exercises itself in speculation merely, and not in action; and if the experiences of purely speculative men were gathered, we think that most of them would be found to confess, bitterly confess, that indulgence in an abstract reflective thinking (whatever effect it may have ultimately upon their nobler genius, supposing them to have one) in the meantime absolutely kills, or appears to kill, all the minor faculties of the soul— all the lesser genial powers, upon the exercise of which the greater part of human happiness depends. They would own, not without remorse, that pure speculation—that is, knowledge pursued *for itself* alone—has often been tasted by them to be, as Coleridge elsewhere says, 'the bitterest and rottenest part of the core of the fruit of the forbidden tree.' This seems a strange confession for a thinker reputed so abstract as Ferrier, but of course the truth of what he says is evident. Knowledge regarded as an end in itself might have brought Faust into his troubles, it is true, and he might likewise have found himself ready to rush into what he conceives to be the opposite extreme; but a greater philosopher than Ferrier has said that though 'knowledge brought about the Fall, it also contains the principle of Redemption,' and we take this to signify that we must look at knowledge as a necessary element in the culture and education of an individual or a people, which, though it carries trouble in its wake, does not leave us in our distress, but brings along with it the principle of healing, or is the 'healer of itself.'

Soon after the above, Ferrier contributes to the same journal an article entitled 'The Tittle-Tattle of a Philosopher,' or an account of the 'Journey through Life' of Professor Krug of Leipzig. Krug appears to have been a sort of Admirable Crichton amongst philosophers, to whom no subject came amiss, and who was ready to take his part in every sort of philosophical discussion. By Hegel and the idealist school he is somewhat contemptuously referred to as one of that class of writers of whom it is said '*Ils se sont battus les flancs pour être de grands hommes.*' Anyhow, his recollections are at least amusing, if not philosophically edifying.

A review of the poems of Coventry Patmore a few years later is a very different production. It carries us back to the old days of *Blackwood*, when calm judgment was not so much an object as strength of expression, withering criticism, and biting sarcasm. Ferrier no doubt believed it would be well for literature to turn back to the old days of the knout; but few, we fancy, will agree with him, even if they suffer for so differing by permitting certain trashy publications to see the light. Too often, unfortunately, the knout, when it is applied, arrives on shoulders that are innocent. Of course Ferrier believed that the worst prognostications of a quarter of a century before were now being realised by the application not being persevered in; but as to this particular piece of criticism, whatever our opinion of Patmore's poetic powers may be, surely the writer was unreasonably severe; surely the work does not deserve to be dealt with in such unmeasured terms of opprobrium. It is refreshing to turn to an appreciative, if also somewhat critical review of the poems of Elizabeth Barrett, published in the same year, 1844, part of which has been republished in the *Remains*. In this article Ferrier urges once more the point on which he continually insists—the adoption of a direct simplicity of style: one which goes straight to the point, or, as he puts it, which is felt to 'get through business.' Excepting certain criticism on the score of style and phraseology, however, Ferrier is all praise of the high degree of poetic merit which the writings revealed—merit which he must have been amongst the first to discover and make known.

The last of Ferrier's work for the magazine in which he had so often written, was a series of articles on the New Readings from Shakespeare, published in 1853. These articles were in the main a criticism of Mr. Payne Collier's 'Notes and Emendations' to the Text of Shakespeare's 'Plays' from early MS. corrections which he had discovered in a copy of the folio 1632. Ferrier, who was a thorough Shakespeare student, and whose appreciation of Shakespeare is often spoken of by those who knew him, had no faith in the authenticity of the new readings, though he thinks they have a certain interest as matter of curiosity. He goes through the plays and the alterations made in them *seriatim*, and comes to the conclusion that in most cases they have little value. In fact, he proceeds so far as to say that they have opened his eyes to 'a depth of purity and correctness in the received text of Shakespeare' of which he had no suspicion—a satisfactory conclusion to the ordinary reader.

Besides his work for *Blackwood*, Ferrier was in the habit of contributing articles to the *Imperial Dictionary of Universal Biography* on the various philosophers. Two of these, the biographies of Schelling and Hegel, are printed in the *Remains*, but besides these he wrote on Adam Smith, Swift, Schiller, etc., and occasionally utilised the articles in his lectures.

On yet another line Ferrier wrote a pamphlet in 1848, entitled *Observations on Church and State*, suggested by the Duke of Argyll's essay on the Ecclesiastical History of Scotland. This pamphlet aims at proving that the Assembly of the Church is really, as the Duke argues, not merely an ecclesiastical, but a national council, or, as Ferrier terms it, the 'second and junior of the Scottish Houses of Parliament.' Being therefore amenable to no other earthly power, it was justified in opposing the decrees of the Court of Session; though, however, the Free Church ministers were right in defending their constitutional privileges, Ferrier holds that they were wrong in doing so as the 'Church' in opposition to the 'State,' and that this brought upon them their discomfiture. They should not, in his view, have acknowledged that the Church's property could be forfeit to the State, and consequently should not have voluntarily resigned their livings. The pamphlet shows considerable interest in the controversy raging so vehemently at the time.

In St. Andrews there was no social meeting at which Ferrier was not a welcome guest. When popular lectures, then coming into vogue, were instituted in the town, Ferrier was called upon to deliver one of the series, the subject chosen being 'Our Contemporary Poetical Literature.' He says in a letter: 'I am in perfect agony in quest of something to say about "Our Contemporary Poets" in the Town Hall here on Friday. I must pump up something, being committed like an ass to that subject, but devil a thing will come. I wish Aytoun would come over and plead their cause.' However, in spite of fears, the lecture appears to have been a success: it was an eloquent appeal on behalf of poetry as an invaluable educational factor and agent in carrying forward the work of human civilisation, and an appreciation of the work of Tennyson, Macaulay, Aytoun, and Lytton. In the same year, but a few months later, Ferrier was asked to deliver the opening address of the Edinburgh Philosophical Institution. This Institution has for long been the means of bringing celebrities from all parts of the country to lecture before an Edinburgh audience, and its origin and conception was largely due to Professor Wilson, Ferrier's father-in-law, who was in the habit of opening the session with an introductory address. His health no longer permitting this to be done, the directors requested Ferrier to take his place. The address was on purely general topics, dealing mainly with the objects of the Institution, then somewhat of a novelty. He concluded: 'Labour is the lot of man. No pleasure can surpass the satisfaction which a man feels in the efficient discharge of the active duties of his calling. But it is equally true that every professional occupation, from the highest to the lowest, requires to be counterpoised and alleviated by pursuits of a more liberal order than itself. Without these the best faculties of our souls must sink down into an ignoble torpor, and human intercourse be shorn of its highest enjoyments, and its brightest blessings.' This is characteristic of Ferrier's view of life. One-sidedness was his particular abhorrence, and if he could in any measure impress its evil upon those whose daily business was apt to engross their attention, to the detriment of the higher spheres of thinking, he was glad at least to make the attempt.

CHAPTER VIII

PROFESSORIAL LIFE

The St. Andrews University has the reputation of being given to strife, and never being thoroughly at rest unless it has at least one law-plea in operation before the Court of Session in Edinburgh, or an appeal before the House of

Lords in London. In a small town, and more especially in a small University town, there is of course unlimited opportunity for discussing every matter of interest, and battles are fought and won before our very doors—battles often just as interesting as those of the great world outside, and more engrossing because in them we probably play the part of active participators, instead of being simple spectators from outside. Of this time Sheriff Smith, however, writes: 'Never was the University set more social, and less given to strife than in Ferrier's day. Grander feats I have often seen elsewhere, but brighter or more intellectual talk, ranging from the playful to the profound, never have I heard anywhere.' In this respect it contrasts with the more self-conscious and less natural social gatherings of the neighbouring city of Edinburgh, whose stiffness and formality was unknown to the smaller town. The company, without passing beyond University bounds, was excellent. There was Tulloch at St. Mary's, still a young man at his prime, and a warm friend of Ferrier's in spite of the traditional decree that St. Mary's dealings with the other College should be as few as might be; there was Shairp, afterwards Professor of Poetry in Oxford, and always a delightful and inspiring companion; in the Chair of Logic there was Professor Spalding, whose ill-health alone prevented him from sharing largely in the social life; and he was succeeded by Professor Veitch, afterwards of Glasgow, whose appreciation of Ferrier was keen, and with whom Ferrier had so much intercourse of a mutually enjoyable sort. Then there was Professor Sellar, a staunch friend and true, and likewise Sir David Brewster, the veteran man of science, whom Scotland delights to honour. When Brewster resigned the Principalship of the United College in 1859, Ferrier was pressed to become a candidate for the post, and Brewster himself promised his support, and urged Ferrier's claims; but there were difficulties in the way, and his place was filled by another follower of science, Principal Forbes.

Ferrier's students are now, of course, dispersed abroad far and wide. One of their number, Sheriff Campbell Smith of Dundee, writes of them as follows:— 'His old students are scattered everywhere—through all countries, professions, and climates. To many of them the world of faith and action has become more narrow and less ideal than it seemed when they sat listening to his lofty and eloquent speculations in the little old classroom among earnest young faces that are no longer young, and nearly all grown dim to memory; but to none of them can there be any feeling regarding him alien to respect and affection, while to many there will remain the conviction that he was for them and their experience the *first* impersonation of living literature, whose lectures, set off by his thrilling voice, slight interesting burr, and solemn pauses, and holding in solution profound original thought and subtle critical suggestions, were a sort of revelation, opening up new worlds, and shedding a flood of new light upon the old familiar world of thought and knowledge in which genius alone could see and disclose wonders.' And this sometime student tells how in passages from the standard poets undetected meanings were discovered, and new light was thrown upon the subject of his talk by quotations from the classics, from Milton and Byron as well as from his favourite Horace. His eloquence, he tells us, might not be so strong and overwhelming as that of Chalmers, but it was more fine, subtle, and poetical in its affinities, revealing thought more splendid and transcendental. 'In person and manner Professor Ferrier was the very ideal of a Professor and a gentleman. Nature had made him in the body what he strove after in spirit. His features were cast in the finest classic mould, and were faultlessly perfect, as was also his tall thin person,—from the finely formed head, thickly covered with black hair, which the last ten years turned into iron-grey, to the noticeably handsome foot.... A human being less under the influence of low or selfish motives could not be conceived in this mercenary anti-ideal age. If he made mistakes, they were due to his living in an ideal world, and not to either malice or guile, both of which were entirely foreign to his nature.'[11] And yet there was nothing of the Puritan about the Professor's nature. There are celebrations in St. Andrews in commemoration of a certain damsel, Kate Kennedy by name, which are characterised by demonstrations of a somewhat noisy order. Some of the Professors denounced this institution and demanded its abolition. But Ferrier had too much sense of humour to do this; he did not rebuke the lads for the exuberance of their spirits, but by his calm dignity contrived to keep them within due bounds.

A picture of Ferrier was painted about a year before his death by Sir John Watson Gordon, and it may still be seen in the University Hall beside the other men of learning who have adorned their University. It was painted for his friends and former students, but though a fairly accurate likeness, it is said not to have conveyed to others the keen, intellectual look so characteristic of the face. It was the nameless charm—charm of manner and personality—that drew Ferrier's students so forcibly towards him. As his colleague, Principal Tulloch, said in a lecture after his death: 'There was a buoyant and graceful charm in all he did—a perfect sympathy, cordiality, and frankness which won the hearts of his students as of all who sought his intellectual companionship. Maintaining the dignity of his position with easy indifference, he could descend to the most free and affectionate intercourse; make his students as it were parties with him in his discussions, and, while guiding them with a master hand, awaken at the same time their own activities of thought as fellow-workers with himself. There was nothing, I am sure, more valuable in his teaching than this—nothing for which his students will longer remember it with gratitude. No man could be more free from the small vanity of making disciples. He loved speculation too dearly for itself—he prized too highly the sacred right of reason, to wish any man or any student merely to adopt his system or repeat his thought. Not to manufacture thought for others, but to excite thought in others; to stimulate the powers of inquiry, and brace all the higher functions of the intellect, was his great aim. He might be comparatively careless, therefore, of the small process of drilling, and minute labour of correction. These, indeed, he greatly valued in their own place. But he felt that his strength lay in a different direction—in the intellectual impulse which his own thinking, in its life, its zealous and clear open candour, was capable of imparting.'

Ferrier was not, perhaps, naturally endowed with any special capacity for business, but the business that fell to him as a member of the *Senatus Academicus* was performed with the greatest care and zeal. With the movement for women's University education, which has always been to the front in St. Andrews, he was sympathetic, although it was not a matter in which he played any special part. 'No one,' it was said, 'had clearer perceptions or a cooler and fairer judgment in any matter which seemed to him of importance.' Principal Tulloch tells how on one occasion in particular, where the interests of the University were at stake, his clear sense and vigilance carried it through its troubles. His loyalty to St. Andrews at all times was indeed unquestioned. It is possible that had he made it his endeavour to devote more interest to practical affairs outside the University limits, it might have been better for himself. There may, perhaps, be truth in the saying that metaphysics is apt to have an enervating effect upon the moral senses, or at least upon the practical activities, and to take from men's usefulness in the ordinary affairs of life; but one can hardly realise Ferrier other than he was, a student whose whole interests were devoted to the philosophy he had espoused, and who loved to deal with the fundamental questions that remained beneath all action and all thought, rather than with those more concrete; and the former lay in a region purely speculative. Such as he was, he never failed to preserve the most perfect order in his class, and to do what was required of him with praiseworthy accuracy and minute attention to details.

'Life in his study,' says Principal Tulloch, 'was Professor Ferrier's characteristic life. There have been, I daresay, even in our time, harder students than he was; but there could scarcely be anyone who was more habitually a student, who lived more amongst books, and took more special and constant delight in intercourse with them. In his very extensive but choice library he knew every book by head-mark, as he would say, and could lay his hands upon the desired volume at once. It was a great pleasure to him to bring to the light from an obscure corner some comparatively unknown English speculator of whom the University library knew nothing.'

We are often told how he would be found seated in his library clad in a long dressing-gown which clung round his tall form, and making him look even taller—a typical philosopher, though perhaps handsomer than many of his craft. 'My father rarely went from home,' writes his daughter, 'and when not in the College class-room was to be found in his snug, well-stocked, ill-bound library, writing or reading, clad in a very becoming dark blue dressing-gown. He was no smoker, but carried with him a small silver snuff-box.'

Professor Shairp says that now and then he used to go to hear him lecture. 'I never saw anything better than his manner towards his students. There was in it ease, yet dignity so respectful both to them and to himself that no one could think of presuming with him. Yet it was unusually kindly, and full of a playful humour which greatly attached them to him. No one could be farther removed from either the Don or the Disciplinarian. But his look of keen intellect and high breeding, combined with gentleness and feeling for his students, commanded attention more than any discipline could have done. In matters of College discipline, while he was fair and just, he always leant to the forbearing side.... Till his illness took a more serious form, he was to be met at dinner-parties, to which his society always gave a great charm. In general society his conversation was full of humour and playful jokes, and he had a quick yet kindly eye to note the extravagances and absurdities of men.' And the Professor goes on to narrate how on a winter afternoon he would fall to talking of Horace, an especial favourite of his, and how then he would read the racy and unconventional translation he had made up for amusement. And afterwards he would talk of Wordsworth and the feelings he awoke in him, showing 'a richness of literary knowledge, and a delicacy and keenness of appreciation, of which his philosophical writings, except by their fine style, give no hint.' Hegel and Plato were the favourite objects of his study. Of the former he never satisfied himself that he had completely mastered the conception. But the insight that he had got into his dialectic and into the doctrine of Reality contributed very largely to making his philosophy what it was. He endeavoured to apply the system in various directions, and ever continued in his efforts to work it out more fully.

Another former student, who has been quoted before, writes in his Recollections of student life at St. Andrews:[12] 'Ferrier had not Spalding's thorough method of teaching. He had no regular time for receiving and correcting essays; he had only one written examination; for oral examination he had an easy way, in which the questions suggested the answers; yet all these drawbacks were atoned for by his living presence. It was an embodiment of literary and philosophical enthusiasm, happily blended with sympathy and urbanity. It did the work of the most thorough class drill, for it arrested the attention, opened the mind, and filled it with love of learning and wisdom. Intellect and humanity seemed to radiate from his countenance like light and heat, and illumined and fascinated all on whom they fell…. Let me recall him as he appeared in the spring of 1854. The eleven-o'clock bell has rung. All the other classes have gone in to lecture. We, the students of Moral Philosophy, are lingering in the quadrangle, for the Professor, punctual in his unpunctuality, comes in regularly two or three minutes after the hour. Through the archway under the time-honoured steeple of St. Salvator's he approaches—a tall somewhat emaciated figure, with intellectual and benevolent countenance. As he hurries in we follow and take our seats. In a minute he issues gowned from his anteroom, seats himself in his chair, and places his silver snuff-box before him. Now that he is without his hat and in his gown, he has a striking appearance. His head is large, well-developed, and covered with thick iron-grey hair; his features are regular, his mouth is refined and sensitive, his chin is strong, and his eyes as seen behind his spectacles are keenly intelligent and at the same time benevolent. He begins by calling up a student to be orally examined; and the catechising goes on very much in the following style:—

'*Professor.*—Well, Mr. Brown, answer a few questions, if you please. What is the first proposition of the lectures?

'*Student* repeats it.

'*Professor.*—Quite right, Mr. Brown. And, Mr. Brown, is this quite true?

'*Stud.*—Yes.

'*Prof.*—Quite right, Mr. Brown. At least, so I think. And, Mr. Brown, is it not absurd to hold the reverse?

"'*Stud.*—Yes.

"'*Prof.*—Yes, yes. Thank you, Mr. Brown. That will do."

'The Professor then begins his lecture. As long as he is stating and proving the propositions in his metaphysical system, his tone is simple and matter-of-fact. His great aim is to make his meaning plain, and for that purpose he often expresses an important idea in various ways, using synonyms, and sometimes reading a sentence twice. But when he comes to illustrate his thoughts, his manner changes. He lets loose his fancy, his imagination, and even his humour; and his whole soul comes into his voice. His burr, scarcely distinguishable in his ordinary speech, now becomes strong, and his whole utterance is slow, intense, and fervid. He is particularly happy in his quotations from the poets, and he has a peculiarity in reading them which increases the effect. When rolling forth a line he sometimes pauses before he comes to the end, as if to collect his strength, and then utters the last word or words with redoubled emphasis. The effect of his eloquence on the students is electrical. They cease to take notes; every head is raised; every face beams with delight; and at the end of a passage their feelings find vent in a thunderstorm of applause.

'The two most remarkable features of his lectures were their method and clearness. Order and light were the very elements in which his mind lived and moved. He kept this end in view, threw aside the facts that were unnecessary, arranged the facts that were necessary, and expressed them with a precision about which there could be no ambiguity. In fact, each idea and the whole chain of ideas were visible by their own light. So perspicuous were the words that they might have been called crystallised thoughts.

'Out of the classroom Ferrier was equally polite and kind, especially to those students who showed a love and a capacity for philosophy. It was no uncommon thing for him to stop a student in the street and invite him to the house to have a talk about the work of the class. I have a distant recollection of my first visit to his study; I see him yet, with his noble, benignant countenance, as he reads and discusses passages in my first essay, gravely reasoning with me on the points that were reasonable, passing lightly over those that were merely rhetorical, and smiling good-naturedly at those that attacked in no measured language his own system.'

Professor Ferrier was never failing in hospitality to his students as to his other friends. Dr. Pryde goes on: 'Every year Ferrier invited the best of his students to dinner. At the dinner at which I was present there were two of his fellow-professors, Sellar and Fischer. It was a great treat for a youth like me. Mrs. Ferrier was effervescent with animal spirits and talk; Ferrier himself, looking like a nobleman in his old-fashioned dress-coat with gold buttons, interposed occasionally with his subtle touches of wit and humour.' The Professor appears to have been an inveterate snuffer. His students used to tell how the silver snuff-box was made the medium of explaining the Berkeleian system, and how to their minds the system, fairly clear in words, became a hopeless tangle when the assistance of the snuff-box was resorted to. And Dr. Pryde narrates how he used to see Professor Spalding and Professor Ferrier seated side by side in the students' benches, looking on the same book, listening to their young colleague

Professor Sellar's inspiring lectures, and at intervals exchanging snuff-boxes. He gives the following account of his last visit to Ferrier, when he was on his deathbed, but still in his library among his books: 'He told me that his disease was mortal; but face to face with death he was cheerful and contented, and had bated not one jot of his interest in learning and in public events. He was very anxious that I should take lunch with Mrs. Ferrier and the rest of the family; and though he could not join us, he sent into the dining-room a special bottle of wine as a substitute for himself. Two months afterwards he had passed away.'

Tulloch writes after the sad event had occurred:[13] 'I have, of course, heard the sad news from St. Andrews. What sadness it has been to me I cannot tell you. St. Andrews never can be the same place without Ferrier. God knows what is to become of the University with all these breaks upon its old society; and where can we supply such a place as Ferrier's?' And his biographer adds: 'The removal of that delicate and clear spirit from a little society in which his position was so important, and his innate refinement of mind so powerful and beneficial an influence, was a loss almost indescribable, not only to the friends who loved him, but to the University. His great reputation was an honour to the place, combining as it did so many associations of the brilliant past with that due to the finest intellectual perception and the most engaging and attractive character. Even his little whimsicalities and strain of quaint humour gave a charm the more; and the closing of the cheerful house, the centre of wit and brightness to the academical community, was a loss which St. Andrews never failed to feel, nor the survivors to lament.'

Professor Ferrier was occasionally called upon to make a visit to London, although this did not seem to have been by any means a frequent occurrence. Business he must occasionally have had there, for in 1861 he was appointed to examine in the London University, and in 1863, shortly before his death, the Society of Arts offered him an examinership in Logic and Mental Science, in place of the late Archbishop of York, which he accepted. But of one visit which he paid in 1858, with Principal Tulloch as joint delegate from the University of St. Andrews, Mrs. Oliphant gives an amusing account, in her *Memoir of Principal Tulloch*.[14] The object of the deputation was to watch the progress of the University Bill through the House of Commons. This Bill was one of the earliest efforts after regulating the studies, degrees, etc., of the Scottish Universities, and also dealt with an increase in the Parliamentary grant which, if it passed, would considerably affect the Professors' incomes as well as the resources of the University. The Bill, which was under the charge of Lord Advocate Inglis (afterwards Lord Justice-General of Scotland), likewise provided that in each University a University Court should be established, as also a University Council composed of graduates. Ferrier and Tulloch no doubt did their part in the business which they had in hand: they visited all the Members of Parliament who were likely to be interested, as other Scottish deputations have done before and since, and received the same evasive and varying replies. But in the evenings, and when they were free, they entertained themselves in different fashion. First of all, they have hardly arrived after their long night's journey's travel before they burst upon the 'trim and well-ordered room where Mr. John Blackwood and his wife were seated at breakfast'—this evidently at Ferrier's instigation. Then, having settled in Duke Street, St. James's, they are asked, rather inappropriately, it would seem, to a ball, where they were 'equally impressed by the size of the crinoline and the absence of beauty.' Next Cremorne was visited, Tulloch declaring that his object was to take care of his companion. 'If you had seen Ferrier as he gazed frae him with the half-amused, half-scowling expression he not unfrequently assumes, looking bored, and yet with a vague philosophical interest at the wonderful expanse of gay dresses and fresh womanhood around him!' 'He will go nowhere without a cab; to-day for the first time I got him into an omnibus in search of an Aberdeen Professor, a wild and wandering distance which we thought we never should reach.' The theatre was visited, too; Lear was being played, very possibly by Charles Kean. In the Royal Academy, Frith's Derby Day was the attraction of the year. But quite remarkable was the interest which Ferrier—who did not appreciate in general 'going to church,' and used to say he preferred to sit and listen to the faint sounds of the organ from the quiet of his room—betrayed in the eloquence of Spurgeon, then at the height of his fame and attracting enormous congregations round him in the Surrey Garden Theatre. Tulloch wrote to his wife: 'We have just been to hear Spurgeon, and have been both so much impressed that I write to give you my impressions while they are fresh. As we came out we both confessed, "There is no doubt about *that*," and I was struck with Ferrier's remarkable expression, "I feel it would do me good to hear the like of that, it sat so close to reality." The sermon is about the most real thing I have come in contact with for a long time.' The building was large and airy, with window-doors from which you could walk into the gardens beyond, and Ferrier, Tulloch writes, now and then took a turn in the fresh air outside while the sermon was progressing.

After London, Oxford was visited, and here the friends lived at Balliol with Mr. Jowett, who had not yet become the Master. Ferrier would doubtless delight in showing to his friend the beauties of the place with which he had so many memories, but to attend eight-o'clock chapel with Tulloch was, the latter tells us, beyond the limits of his zeal. Just before this, in 1857, another visit was paid by Ferrier to Oxford with his family, and this time to visit Lady Grant, the mother of his future son-in-law. It was at Commemoration-time, we are told, and a ball was given in honour of the party. On this occasion Ferrier for the first time met Professor Jowett, besides many other kindred spirits, and he thoroughly enjoyed wandering about the old haunts at Magdalen, where in his youth he had pelted the deer and played the part of a young and thoughtless gownsman.

A little book was published some years ago, on behoof of the St. Andrews Students' Union, entitled *Speculum Universitatis*, in which former students and *alumni* piously record their recollections of their *Alma Mater*. Some of these papers bring before us very vividly the sort of impression which the life left upon the lads, drawn together from all manner of home surroundings, and equally influenced by the memories of the past and the living presence of those who were the means of opening up new tracts of knowledge to their view. One of them, already often quoted, says in a paper called 'The Light of Long Ago': 'I always sink into the conviction that the St. Andrews United College was never so well worth attending as during the days when in its classrooms Duncan taught Mathematics, Spalding taught Logic, and Ferrier taught Metaphysics and Moral Science, illustrating living literature in his literary style, and in the strange tones, pauses, and inflections of his voice. To the field of literature and speculation Ferrier restored glimpses of the sunshine of Paradise. Under his magical spell they ceased to look like fields that had been cursed with weeds, watered with sweat and tears, and levelled and planted with untold labour. Every utterance of his tended alike to disclose the beauty and penetrate the mystery of existence. He was a persevering philosopher, but he was also a poet by a gift of nature. The burden of this most unintelligible world did not oppress him, nor any other burden. Intellectual action proving the riddles of reason was a joy to him. He loved philosophy and poetry for their own sake, and he infected others with a kindred, but not an equal, passion. He could jest and laugh and play. If he ever discovered that much study is a weariness of the flesh, he most effectually concealed that discovery.'

And to conclude, we have the testimony of another former student who is now distinguished in the fields of literature, but who always remains faithful to his home of early days. Mr. Andrew Lang says: 'Professor Ferrier's lectures on Moral Philosophy were the most interesting and inspiriting that I ever listened to either at Oxford or St. Andrews. I looked on Mr. Ferrier with a kind of mysterious reverence, as on the last of the golden chain of great philosophers. There was, I know not what of dignity, of humour, and of wisdom in his face; there was an air of the student, the vanquisher of difficulties, the discoverer of hidden knowledge, in him that I have seen in no other. His method at that time was to lecture on the History of Philosophy, and his manner was so persuasive that one believed firmly in the tenets of each school he described, till he advanced those of the next! Thus the whole historical evolution of thought went on in the mind of each of his listeners.'

CHAPTER IX

LIFE AT ST. ANDREWS

In an old-world town like St. Andrews the stately, old-world Moral Philosophy Professor must have seemed wonderfully in his place. There are men who, good-looking in youth, become 'ordinary-looking' in later years, but Ferrier's looks were not of such a kind. To the last—of course he was not an old man when he died—he preserved the same distinguished appearance that we are told marked him out from amongst his fellows while still a youth. The tall figure, clad in old-fashioned, well-cut coat and white duck trousers, the close-shaven face, and merry twinkle about the eye signifying a sense of humour which removed him far from anything which we associate with the name of pedant; the dignity, when dignity was required, and yet the sympathy always ready to be extended to the student, however far he was from taking up the point, if he were only trying his best to comprehend—all this made up to those who knew him, the man, the scholar, and the high-bred gentleman, which, in no ordinary or conventional sense, Professor Ferrier was. It is the personality which, when years have passed and individual traits have been forgotten, it is so difficult to reproduce. The personal attraction, the atmosphere of culture and chivalry, which was always felt to hang about the Professor, has not been forgotten by those who can recall him in the old St. Andrews days; but who can reproduce this charm, or do more than state its existence as a fact? Perhaps this sort only comes to those whose life is mainly intellectual—who have not much, comparatively speaking, to suffer from the rough and tumble to which the 'practical' man is subjected in the course of his career. Sometimes it is said that those who preach high maxims of philosophy and conduct belie their doctrines in their outward lives; but on the whole, when we review their careers, this would wonderfully seldom seem to be the case. From Socrates' time onwards we have had philosophers who have taught virtue and practised it simultaneously, and in no case has this combination been better exemplified in recent days than in that of James Frederick Ferrier, and one who unsuccessfully contested his chair upon his death, Thomas Hill Green, Professor of Moral Philosophy at Oxford. It seems as though it may after all be good to speculate on the deep things of the earth as well as to do the deeds of righteousness.

If the saying is true, that the happiest man is he who is without a history, then Ferrier has every claim to be enrolled in the ranks of those who have attained their end. For happiness *was* an end to Ferrier: he had no idea of practising virtue in the abstract, and finding a sufficiency in this. He believed, however, that the happiness to be sought for was the happiness of realising our highest aims, and the aim he put before him he very largely succeeded in attaining. His life was what most people would consider monotonous enough: few events outside the ordinary occurrences of family and University life broke in upon its tranquil course. Unlike the custom of some of his colleagues, summer and winter alike were passed by Ferrier in the quaint old sea-bound town. He lived there largely for his work and books. Not that he disliked society; he took the deepest interest even in his dinner-parties, and whether as a host or as a guest, was equally delightful as a companion or as a talker. But in his books he found his real life; he would take them down to table, and bed he seldom reached till midnight was passed by two hours at least. One who knew and cared for him, the attractive wife of one of his colleagues, who spent ten sessions at St. Andrews before distinguishing the Humanity Chair in Edinburgh, tells how the West Park house had something about its atmosphere that marked it out as unique—something which was due in great measure to the cultured father, but also to the bright and witty mother and the three beautiful young daughters, who together formed a household by itself, and one which made the grey old town a different place to those who lived in it.

Ferrier, as we have seen, had many distinguished colleagues in the University. Besides Professor Sellar, who held the Chair of Greek, there was the Principal of St. Mary's (Principal Tulloch), Professor Shairp, then Professor of Latin, and later on the Principal; the Logic Professor, Veitch, Sir David Brewster, Principal of the United Colleges, and others. But the society was unconventional in the extreme. The salaries were not large: including fees, the ordinance of the

Scottish Universities Commission appointing the salaries of Professors in 1861, estimates the salary of the professorship of Moral Philosophy at St. Andrews at £444, 18s., and the Principal only received about £100 more. But there were not those social customs and conventions to maintain that succeed in making life on a small income irksome in a larger city. All were practically on the same level in the University circle, and St. Andrews was not invaded by so large an army of golfing visitors then as now, though the game of course was played with equal keenness and enthusiasm. Professor Ferrier took no part in this or other physical amusement: possibly it had been better for him had he left his books and study at times to do so. The friend spoken of above tells, however, of the merry parties who walked home after dining out, the laughing protests which she made against the Professor's rash statement (in allusion to his theory of *perception-mecum*) that *she* was 'unredeemed nonsense' without *him*; the way in which, when an idea struck him, he would walk to her house with his daughter, regardless of the lateness of the hour, and throw pebbles at the lighted bedroom windows to gain admittance—and of course a hospitable supper; how she, knowing that a tablemaid was wanted in the Ferrier establishment, dressed up as such and interviewed the mistress, who found her highly satisfactory but curiously resembling her friend Mrs. Sellar; and how when this was told her husband, he exclaimed, 'Why, of course it's she dressed up; let us pursue her,' which was done with good effect! All these tales, and many others like them, show what the homely, sociable, and yet cultured life was like—a life such as we in this country seldom have experience of: perhaps that of a German University town may most resemble it. In spite of being in many ways a recluse, Ferrier was ever a favourite with his students, just because he treated them, not with familiarity indeed, but as gentlemen like himself. Other Professors were cheered when they appeared in public, but the loudest cheers were always given to Ferrier.

Mrs. Ferrier's brilliant personality many can remember who knew her during her widowhood in Edinburgh. She had inherited many of her father, 'Christopher North's' physical and mental gifts, shown in looks and wit. A friend of old days writes: 'She was a queen in St. Andrews, at once admired for her wit, her eloquence, her personal charms, and dreaded for her free speech, her powers of ridicule, and her withering mimicry. Faithful, however, to her friends, she was beloved by them, and they will lament her now as one of the warmest-hearted and most highly-gifted of her sex.' Mrs. Ferrier never wrote for publication,— she is said to have scorned the idea,—but those who knew her never can forget the flow of eloquence, the wit and satire mingled, the humorous touches and the keen sense of fun that characterised her talk; for she was one of an era of brilliant talkers that would seem to have passed away. Mrs. Ferrier's capacity for giving appropriate nicknames was well known: Jowett, afterwards Master of Balliol, she christened the 'little downy owl.' Her husband's philosophy she graphically described by saying that 'it made you feel as if you were sitting up on a cloud with nothing on, a lucifer match in your hand, but nothing to strike it on,'—a description appealing vividly to many who have tried to master it!

In many ways she seemed a link with the past of bright memories in Scotland, when these links were very nearly severed. Five children in all were born to her;

of her sons one, now dead, inherited many of his father's gifts. Her elder daughter, Lady Grant, the wife of Sir Alexander Grant, Principal of the Edinburgh University and a distinguished classical scholar, likewise succeeded to much of her mother's grace and charm as well as of her father's accomplishments. Under the initials 'O. J.' she was in the habit of contributing delightful humorous sketches to *Blackwood's Magazine*—the magazine which her father and her grandfather had so often contributed to in their day; but her life was not a long one: she died in 1895, eleven years after her husband, and while many possibilities seemed still before her.

Perhaps we might try to picture to ourselves the life in which Ferrier played so prominent a part in the only real University town of which Scotland can boast. For it is in St. Andrews that the traditional distinctions between the College and the University are maintained, that there is the solemn stillness which befits an ancient seat of learning, that every step brings one in view of some monument of ages that are past and gone, and that we are reminded not only of the learning of our ancestors, of their piety and devotion to the College they built and endowed, but of the secular history of our country as well. In this, at least, the little University of the North has an advantage over her rich and powerful rivals, inasmuch as there is hardly any important event which has taken place in Scottish history but has left its mark upon the place. No wonder the love of her students to the *Alma Mater* is proverbial. In Scotland we have little left to tell us of the mediæval church and life, so completely has the Reformation done its work, and so thoroughly was the land cleared of its 'popish images'; and hence we value what little there remains to us all the more. And the University of St. Andrews, the oldest of our seats of learning, has come down to us from mediæval days. It was founded by a Catholic bishop in 1411, about a century after the dedication of the Cathedral, now, of course, a ruin. But it is to the good Bishop Kennedy who established the College of St. Salvator, one of the two United Colleges of later times, that we ascribe most honour in reference to the old foundation. Not only did he build the College on the site which was afterwards occupied by the classrooms in which Ferrier and his colleagues taught, but he likewise endowed them with vestments and rich jewels, including amongst their numbers a beautifully chased silver mace which may still be seen. Of the old College buildings there is but the chapel and janitor's house now existing; within the chapel, which is modernised and used for Presbyterian service, is the ancient founder's tomb. The quadrangle, after the Reformation, fell into disrepair, and the present buildings are comparatively of recent date. The next College founded—that of St. Leonard—which became early imbued with Reformation principles, was, in the eighteenth century, when its finances had become low, incorporated with St. Salvator's, and when conjoined they were in Ferrier's time, as now, known as the 'United College.' Besides the United College there was a third and last College, called St. Mary's. Though founded by the last of the Catholic bishops before the Reformation, it was subsequently presided over by the anti-prelatists Andrew Melville and Samuel Rutherford. St. Mary's has always been devoted to the study of theology.

But the history of her colleges is not all that has to be told of the ancient city. Association it has with nearly all who have had to do with the making of our history—the good Queen Margaret, Beaton, and, above all, Queen Mary and her great opponent Knox. The ruined Castle has many tales to tell could stones and trees have tongues—stories of bloodshed, of battle, of the long siege when Knox was forced to yield to France and be carried to the galleys. After the murder of Archbishop Sharp, and the revolution of 1688, the town once so prosperous dwindled away, and decayed into an unimportant seaport. There is curiously little attractive about its situation in many regards. It is out of the way, difficult of access once upon a time, and even now not on a main line of rail, too near the great cities, and yet at the same time too far off. The coast is dangerous for fishermen, and there is no harbour that can be called such. No wonder, it seems, that the town became neglected and insanitary, that Dr. Johnson speaks of 'the silence and solitude of inactive indigence and gloomy depopulation,' and left it with 'mournful images.' But if St. Andrews had its drawbacks, it had still more its compensations. It had its links—the long stretch of sandhills spread far along the coast, and bringing crowds of visitors to the town every summer as it comes round; and for the pursuit of learning the remoteness of position has some advantages. Even at its worst the University showed signs of its recuperative powers. Early in the century Chalmers was assistant to the Professor of Mathematics, and then occupied the Chair of Moral Philosophy (that chair to which Ferrier was afterwards appointed), and drew crowds of students round him. Then came a time of innovation. If in 1821 St. Andrews was badly paved, ill-lighted, and ruinous, an era of reform set in. New classrooms were built, the once neglected library was added to and rearranged, and the town was put to rights through an energetic provost, Major, afterwards Sir Hugh, Lyon Playfair. He made 'crooked places straight' in more senses than one, swept away the 'middens' that polluted the air, saw to the lighting and paving of the streets, and generally brought about the improvements which we expect to find in a modern town. 'On being placed in the civic chair, he had found the streets unpaved, uneven, overgrown with weeds, and dirty; the ruins of the time-honoured Cathedral and Castle used as a quarry for greedy and sacrilegious builders, and the University buildings falling into disrepair; and he had resolved to change all this. With persistency almost unexampled, he had employed all the arts of persuasion and compulsion upon those who had the power to remedy these abuses. He had dunned, he had coaxed, he had bantered, he had bargained, he had borrowed, he had begged; and he had been successful. In 1851 the streets were paved and clean, the fine old ruins were declared sacred, and the dilapidated parts of the University buildings had been replaced by a new edifice. And he—the Major, as he was called—a little man, white-haired, shaggy-eyebrowed, blue-eyed, red-faced, with his hat cocked on the side of his head, and a stout cane in his hand, walked about in triumph, the uncrowned king of the place.'[15]

Of this same renovating provost, it is told that one day he dropped in to see the Moral Philosophy Professor, who, however deeply engaged with his books, was always ready to receive his visitors. 'Well, Major, I have just completed the great

70

work of my life. In this book I claim to make philosophy intelligible to the meanest understanding.' Playfair at once requested to hear some of it read aloud. Ferrier reluctantly started to read in his slow, emphatic way, till the Major became fidgety; still he went on, till Playfair started to his feet. 'I say, Ferrier, do you mean to say this is intelligible to the meanest understanding?' 'Do you understand it, Major?' 'Yes, I think I do.' 'Then, Major, I'm satisfied.'

Of the social life, Mrs. Oliphant says in her *Life of Principal Tulloch*: 'The society, I believe, was more stationary than it has been since, and more entirely disposed to make of St. Andrews the pleasantest and brightest of abiding-places. Sir David Brewster was still throned in St. Leonard's. Professor Ferrier, with his witty and brilliant wife—he full of quiet humour, she of wildest wit, a mimic of alarming and delightful power, with something of the countenance and much of the genius of her father, the great "Christopher North" of *Blackwood's Magazine*—made the brightest centre of social mirth and meetings. West Park, their pleasant home, at the period which I record it, was ever open, ever sounding with gay voices and merry laughter, with a boundless freedom of talk and comment, and an endless stream of good company. Professor Ferrier himself was one of the greatest metaphysicians of his time—the first certainly in Scotland; but this was perhaps less upon the surface than a number of humorous ways which were the delight of his friends, many quaint abstractions proper to his philosophic character, and a happy friendliness and gentleness along with his wit, which gave his society a continual charm.' Professor Knight, who now occupies Ferrier's place in the professoriate of St. Andrews, in his *Life of Professor Shairp*, quotes from a paper of reminiscences by Professor Sellar: 'The centre of all the intellectual and social life of the University and of the town was Professor Ferrier. He inspired in the students a feeling of affectionate devotion as well as admiration, such as I have hardly ever known inspired by any teacher; and to many of them his mere presence and bearing in the classroom was a large element in a liberal education. By all his colleagues he was esteemed as a man of most sterling honour, a staunch friend, and a most humorous and delightful companion.... There certainly never was a household known to either of us in which the spirit of racy and original humour and fun was so exuberant and spontaneous in every member of it, as that of which the Professor and his wife— the most gifted and brilliant, and most like her father of the three gifted daughters of "Christopher North"—were the heads. Our evenings there generally ended in the Professor's study, where he was always ready to discuss, either from a serious or humorous point of view (not without congenial accompaniment), the various points of his system till the morning was well advanced.'

Ferrier's daughter writes of the house at West Park: 'It was an old-fashioned, rough cast or "harled" house standing on the road in Market Street, but approached through a small green gate and a short avenue of trees—trees that were engraven on the heart and memory from childhood. The garden at the back still remains. In our time it was a real old-fashioned Scotch garden, well stocked with "berries," pears, and apples; quaint grass walks ran through it, and a summer-house with stained-glass windows stood in a corner. West Park was built on a site once occupied by the Grey Friars, and I am not romancing when I say that bones and coins were known to have been discovered in the garden even in our time. Our home was socially a very amusing and happy one, though my father lived a good deal apart from us, coming down from his dear old library occasionally in the evenings to join the family circle.' This family circle was occasionally supplemented by a French teacher or a German, and for one year by a certain Mrs. Huggins, an old ex-actress who originally came to give a Shakespeare reading in St. Andrews, and who fell into financial difficulties, and was invited by the hospitable Mrs. Ferrier to make her home for a time at West Park. The visit was not in all respects a success, Mrs. Huggins being somewhat exacting in her requirements and difficult to satisfy. So little part did its master take in household matters that it was only by accident, after reading prayers one Sunday evening, that he noticed her presence. On inquiring who the stranger was, Mrs. Ferrier replied, 'Oh, that is Mrs. Huggins.' 'Then what is her avocation?' 'To read Shakespeare and draw your window-curtains,' said the ever-ready Mrs. Ferrier! The children of the house were brought up to love the stage and everyone pertaining to it, and whenever a strolling company came to St. Andrews the Ferriers were the first to attend their play. The same daughter writes that when children their father used to thrill them with tales of Burke and Hare, the murderers and resurrectionists whose doings brought about a reign of terror in Edinburgh early in the century. As a boy, Ferrier used to walk out to his grandfather's in Morningside—then a country suburb—in fear and trembling, expecting every moment to meet Burke, the object of his terror. On one occasion he believed that he had done so, and skulked behind a hedge and lay down till the scourge of Edinburgh passed by. In 1828 he witnessed his hanging in the Edinburgh prison. Professor Wilson, his father-in-law, it may be recollected, spoke out his mind about the famous Dr. Knox in the *Noctes* as well as in his classroom, and it was a well-known fact that his favourite Newfoundland dog Brontë was poisoned by the students as an act of retaliation.

Murder trials had always a fascination for Ferrier. On one occasion he read aloud to his children De Quincey's essay, 'Murder as a Fine Art,' which so terrified his youngest daughter that she could hardly bring herself to leave her father's library for bed. Somewhat severe to his sons, to his daughters Ferrier was specially kind and indulgent, helping them with their German studies, reading Schiller's plays to them, and when little children telling them old-world fairy tales. A present of Grimm's Tales, brought by her father after a visit to London, was, she tells us, a never-to-be-forgotten joy to the recipient.

The charm of the West Park house was spoken of by all the numerous young men permitted to frequent its hospitable board. There was a wonderful concoction known by the name of 'Bishop,' against whose attraction one who suffered by its potency says that novices were warned, more especially in view of a certain sunk fence in the immediate vicinity which had afterwards to be avoided. The jokes that passed at these entertainments, which were never dull, are past and gone,—their piquancy would be gone even could they be reproduced,—but the impression left on the minds of those who shared in them is ineffaceable, and is as vivid now as forty years ago.

There was a custom, now almost extinct, of keeping books of so-called 'Confessions,' in which the contributors had the rather formidable task of filling up their likes or dislikes for the entertainment of their owners. In Mrs. Sellar's album Ferrier made several interesting 'confessions'—whether we take them *au grand sérieux* or only as playful jests with a grain of truth behind. Here are some of the questions and their answers.

Question.	Answer.
Your favourite character in history.	Socrates.
The character you most dislike.	Calvin.
Your favourite kind of literature.	*The Arabian Nights.*
Your favourite author.	Hegel.
Your favourite occupation and amusement.	Driving with a handsome woman.
Those you dislike most.	Fishing, walking, and dancing.
Your favourite topics of conversation.	Humorous and tender.
Those you dislike most.	Statistical and personal.
Your ambition.	To reach the Truth.
Your ideal.	Always to pay ready money.
Your hobby.	Peacemaking.
The virtue you most admire.	Reasonableness.
The vices to which you are most lenient.	The world, the flesh, and the devil.

These last two answers are very characteristic of Ferrier's point of view in later days. He was above all reasonable—no ascetic who could not understand the temptations of the world, but one who enjoyed its pleasures, saw the humorous side of life, appreciated the æsthetic, and yet kept the dictates of reason ever before his mind. And his ambition to reach the Truth

'Differed from a host
Of aims alike in character and kind,
Mostly in this—that in itself alone
Shall its reward be, not an alien end
Blending therewith.'

Thus, like Paracelsus, he aspired.

CHAPTER X

LAST DAYS

It used to be said that none can be counted happy until they die, and certainly the manner of a man's death often throws light upon his previous life, and enables us to judge it as we should not otherwise have been able to do. Ferrier's death was what his life had been: it was with calm courage that he looked it in the face—the same calm courage with which he faced the perhaps even greater problems of life that presented themselves. Death had no terrors to him; he had lived in the consciousness that it was an essential factor in life, and a factor which was not ever to be overlooked. And he had every opportunity, physically speaking, for expecting its approach. In November 1861 he had a violent seizure of *angina pectoris*, after which, although he temporarily recovered, he never completely regained his strength. For some weeks he was unable to meet his students, and then, when partially recovered, he arranged to hold the class in the dining-room of his house, which was fitted up specially for the purpose. Twice in the year 1863 was he attacked in a similar way; in June of that year he went up to London to conduct the examination in philosophy of the students of the London University; but in October, when he ought to have gone there once more, he was unable to carry out his intention. On the 31st of October, Dr. Christison was consulted about his state, and pronounced his case to be past hope of remedy. He opened his class on the 11th of November in his own house, but during this month was generally confined to bed. On the 8th of December he was attacked by congestion of the brain, and never lectured again. His class was conducted by Mr. Rhoades,[16] then Warden of the recently-founded College Hall, who, as many others among his colleagues would have been ready to do, willingly undertook the melancholy task of officiating for so beloved and honoured a friend. After this, all severe study and mental exertion was forbidden. He became gradually weaker, with glimpses now and then of transitory improvement. So in unfailing courage and resignation, not unwilling to hope for longer respite, but always prepared to die, he placidly, reverently, awaited the close, tended by the watchful care of his devoted wife and children.[17] On the 11th day of June 1864, Ferrier passed away. He is buried in Edinburgh, in the old churchyard of St. Cuthbert's, in the heart of the city, near his father and his grandfather, and many others whose names are famous in the annals of his country.

During these three years, in which death had been a question of but a short time, Ferrier had not ceased to be busy and interested in his work. The dates of his lectures on Greek Philosophy show that he had not failed to carry on the work of bringing them into shape, and though the wish could not be accomplished in its entirety, it speaks much for his resolution and determination that through all his bodily weakness he kept his work in hand. Of course much had to be forgone. Ferrier was never what is called robust, and his manner of life was not conducive to physical health, combining as it did late hours with lack of physical exercise. But in these later years he was unable to walk more than the shortest distance, the ascent of a staircase was an effort to him, and tendencies to asthma developed which must have made his life often enough a physical pain. Still, though it was evident that there could be but one ending to the struggle, Ferrier gave expression to no complaints, and though he might, as Principal Tulloch says, utter a half-playful, half-grim expression regarding his sufferings, he never seemed to think there was anything strange in them, anything that he should not bear calmly as a man and as a Christian. Nor did he talk of change of scene or climate as likely to give relief. He 'quietly, steadily, and cheerfully' faced the issue, be it what it might. The very day before he died, he was, we are told, in his library, busy amongst his books. Truly, it may be said of him as of another cut off while yet in his prime, 'he died learning.'

'Towards his friends during this time,' says his biographer, 'all that was sweetest in his disposition seemed to gain strength and expansion from the near shadow of death. He spoke of death with entire fearlessness, and though this was nothing new to those who knew him best, it impressed their minds at this time more vividly than ever. The less they dared to hope for his life being prolonged, the more their love and regard were deepened by his tender thoughtfulness for others, and the kindliness which annihilated all absorbing concern for himself. In many little characteristic touches of humour, frankness, beneficence, beautiful gratitude for any slight help or attention, his truest and best nature seemed to come out all the more freely; he grew as it were more and more entirely himself indeed. If ever a man was true to philosophy, or a man's philosophy true to him, it was so with Ferrier during all the time when he looked death in the face and possessed his soul in patience.' And, as so often happens when the things of this world are regarded *sub specie æternitatis*, the old animosities, such as they were, faded away. It is told how a former opponent on philosophical questions whose criticisms he had resented, called to inquire for him, and when the card was given to him, Ferrier exclaimed, 'That must be a good fellow!' Principal Tulloch, his friend and for ten years his colleague, was with him constantly, and talked often to him about his work—the work on Plato and his philosophy, that he would have liked to accomplish in order to complete his lectures. The summer before his death they read together some of Plato's dialogues which he had carefully pencilled with his notes. He also took to reading Virgil, in which occupation his friend frequently joined with him, and this seemed to relieve the languor from which he suffered. As to religion, which was a subject on which he thought much, although he did not frequently express an opinion, Tulloch says: 'He was unable to feel much interest in any of its popular forms, but he had a most intense interest in its great mysteries, and a thorough reverence for its truths when these were not disfigured by superstition and formalism.' Immortality, as we have seen, meant to him that there is a permanent and abiding element beyond the merely particular and individual which must pass away, and so far it was a reality in his mind. God was a real presence in the world, and not a far away divinity in whom men believed but whom they could not know; but as to the creeds and doctrines of the Church, they seemed far removed from the Essential, from true Reality. Professor (afterwards Principal) Shairp writes: 'In the visits which I made to his bedroom from time to time, when I found him sometimes on chair or sofa, sometimes in bed, I never heard one peevish or complaining word escape him, nothing but what was calm and cheerful, though to himself as to others it was evident that the outward man was fast perishing. The last time but one that I saw him was on a Sunday in April. He was sitting up in bed. The conversation fell on serious subjects, on the craving the soul feels for some strength and support out from and above itself, on the certainty that all men feel that need, and on the testimony left by those who have tried it most, that they had found that need met by Him of whose earthly life the gospel histories bear witness. This, or something like this, was the subject on which our conversation turned. He paused and dwelt on the thought of the soul's hunger. "Hunger is the great weaver in moral things as in physical. The hunger that is in the new-born child sits weaving the whole bodily frame, bones and sinews, out of nothing. And so I suppose in moral and spiritual things it is hunger that builds up the being.'"

Professor Veitch, a later colleague at St. Andrews, adds: 'We miss the finely-cut decisive face, the erect manly presence, the measured meditative step, the friendly greeting. But there are men, and Ferrier was one of them, for whom, once known, there is no real past. The characteristic features and qualities of such men become part of our conscious life; memory keeps them before us living and influential, in a higher, truer present which overshadows the actual and visible.' And Professor Baynes speaks of him as one of the noblest and most pure-hearted men that he had ever known, combining 'a fine ethereal intelligence with a most gallant, tender, and courageous spirit.'

Such is the man as he presented himself to his friends even when the shadows were darkening and the last long journey coming very near: a true man and a good; one in whose footsteps we fain would tread, one who makes it easier for those who follow him to tread them too. His work was done; it might seem unfinished—what work is ever complete? But he had taken his share in it, the little bit that any individual man can do, and had done it with all his strength. And what did it amount to? Was it worth the labour of so many years of toil? Who is there who can reply? And yet we can see something of what has been accomplished; we can see that philosophy has been made a more living thing for Scotland, that a blow has been struck against materialistic creeds, or beliefs which are merely formal and without any true convincing power. It may not have been much: the work was but begun, and it was left to others to carry that work on. But in philosophy, as in the rest, it is the first step that costs, and amid great difficulty and considerable opposition Ferrier took that step. He left much unexplained; he dwelt too much in the clouds, and did not try to solve the real difficulties of personal, individual life; he did not show how his high-flown theories worked in a world of strife and struggle, of sin and sorrow. He could only be said to have struck a keynote, but that keynote as far as it went was true, and the harmonies may be left to follow.

CPSIA information can be obtained at www.ICGtesting.com
Printed in the USA
LVOW04s1617300415

436757LV00015B/722/P